WHO
CARES ?

CAROLE PARKER

DEDICATION
TO ALL THE PEOPLE WHO SPEND THEIR LIVES CARING FOR OTHERS.

Especially those colleagues in Greater Manchester, who are the inspiration for my writing. They continue to provide a professional service with kindness, compassion and humour.

CONTENTS

ACKNOWLEDGMENTS

To my Family and Friends in the UK and in Syros Greece
for their encouragement, advice and support.

CARLA

In the Beginning….

Suffering produces Endurance, Endurance produces
Character and Character produces Hope.

Romans 5. 3-4

My name is Carla Saxon at forty- two years old, I chose
to build a new career, I hadn't been employed for over ten years.
I was lucky, I was given a second chance, I was the fortunate
recipient of extra time, I was given a new heart. My aim now was
to give something back to society, to make a difference, all the
usual clichés we idealist and optimists hope for. I ventured into
the world of Care, working in the local Community. I have taken
my experience in this work and my own life to try and build a
realistic picture of our society, of people. My characters are
fictional, events, names, places are from my knowledge and
recreated by my imagination.   We are all vulnerable at some
point in our lives, we all ride the roller coaster of events, the pain,

frustration, laughter, jubilation and tears. A wise lady once said to me, "In the tapestry of Life, we need the dark threads, to show us how bright the lighter threads are."

It would be true to say that I have courted death for most of my existence. I was aware from an early age of my vulnerability; my health was always troublesome. In particular I recall from my early years being plagued by chest infections, coughs and breathing issues. Being sent to bed as a very young child with a bag of camphor tied around my neck or later being coated with Vick menthol rub. One morning I remember well, I would have been no older than five, I awoke to find both my eyes completely sealed, I could not open them. The sheer panic I felt, convinced that I was at least blind if not dead! Only my grandfather's reassuring word kept me calm, as he carried me downstairs, then patiently bathed each eye with warm water until my sight was restored. I developed a mild addiction to the delicious cough syrup, with the strong liquorice flavour, often exaggerating the cough for an extra teaspoon full of the dark sweet syrup.

As my body grew and developed so did my health issues. Always a cold child, never keen on outdoor physical activities, preferring the less demanding games where imagination replaced the need for physical exertion. Attempts to teach me to swim were soon abandoned, once I could float without drowning. To actually swim any length was exhausting, my breathing could never keep up with the demands of my body. I suppose upon reflection, it is easy to see why teaching staff had me labeled as "could do better," or "lacks concentration". It's hard to concentrate when your body is demanding sleep, when being last in the race, is always accompanied by discomfort and panting. The issues became more severe as I reached double figures, from the age of eleven I was streamed into the "Sports" channel at secondary school. (Though streaming was deemed politically incorrect at this time, it still took place.) This "House" was noted for always winning at sports, producing the best netball and hockey players, winning the cross country and leading the league with tennis. Of course, breathing is required

10

for all these activities. I found just the walk to the playing fields, which was uphill, physically exhausting. Once there I would find ways not to participate. This of course required certain skills of deception and cunning, which did nothing for my reputation amongst the teaching staff.

During these years I developed my mastery of forgery,writing notes to excuse me from most activities. No one appeared to notice that I was clearly the sickest child in the school. I was extremely inventive from migraines to sprained wrist. The most faithful excuse was my monthly menstruation, which had started early. This could   occur several times a month. Each day I was given a few coppers (the equivalent of around two pence today) this was sufficient to buy a small treat at lunchtime. I saved this money for bus fare to ride home. This excused me from the painful walk uphill, it was lonely, because I could not keep pace with friends, who trotted up the hundred and two ' Fire station Steps', without a pause for breath.

When I became too warm, or there was little air, such as in the school assembly each morning. I would faint. This became a regular feature and was at best treated as an inconvenience, when staff had to guide me out of the hall. Sometimes it was regarded as a deliberate act, to get attention. Then I was scolded, especially if I fell forward onto the unsuspecting girl in front of me, who would scream out, more in shock than pain, at my untimely wobble. I once fainted in the bus station; friend's half carried me to school. We always shared a cigarette before school but this morning I couldn't face it. I had the smell of cigarettes on my clothes, so my punishment was to stand under the clock, when I fell over, I was given a seat.

Academically, I don't suppose I was ever going to be a great scholar. The constant 'day dreaming ' and fight to keep awake were definitely drawbacks, I often lost the thread of what the teachers were saying; so of course, never answered the questions correctly. Mathematics was a nightmare, I struggled with basic principles, the only class I actually enjoyed was art. Due to my rebellious nature I was not allowed an option in my third year. It was basically a choice between Shorthand and

11

Typing, Science or Domestic Science. I didn't feel I was clever enough for science, my cooking and sewing skills were non-existent, so I asked for the secretarial option, I could then aspire to working in an office. This would not be possible I was told, the reason, a friend had already opted for this and the staff felt I would be disruptive to the class, if both friends were together. So, it was Science, chemistry and biology, I was amazed they trusted me, with a Bunsen burner and a scalpel, and allowed me to dissect dead creatures. If it hadn't been for the fact that the science teacher made it perfectly clear she didn't want me in her class, I might have enjoyed science. Indeed, I once scored highly on a project set by an outside body, the teachers only remark was, 'who did this for you'.

My early years in secondary education were plagued by bullying. I had a learned the power of speech so my vocabulary was not exactly charming, I could throw a good insult at anyone. Physically, I usually lost, though it should be noted the bullies never attacked alone, they always had their accomplices to cheer them on, to add the odd push or kick if required. I was never really sure why I was targeted, may be my size? Or my way with words? Certainly, as I grew, my shapely figure and my bravado didn't help. Whatever the reason, it was a lesson in toughening up, so by the third year I had developed bullying skills all of my own, attack being easier than defense.

As I reached my teen years, to conform with my peers, I did the worst thing I could have done. I started smoking cigarettes properly, prior to this I had played at smoking. Just the odd one or two at first, not realising that this would soon become a habit which would take over thirty years to break. It also contributed to an increase in my health problems, though of course I always denied this.

By the age of fourteen my teachers and my family had virtually given up on me. I was trouble. I hardly attended school, I had experimented with alcohol and milder illegal drugs such as weed and LSD. I was sexually aware, I knew all the answers, well at least I thought I did. Finally, the Headteacher announced that she was very pleased I could leave at Easter, having just turned fifteen. I left with my only proof of attendance, the standard school Bible and my well-worn Beret!

I continued through my early teen age years, experiencing various health issues, attacks of breathlessness, fainting and tiredness. I would have to wait until I reached my early thirties to be finally diagnosed and a further ten years before a solution is found. One first love, two marriages, two children, two lost souls. New beginnings, starting over, back to school. A career that ranges from the cotton mills of Lancashire to an Executive Career in the world's busiest airport, through years of medical intervention, bereavement and change. To unemployment and financial chaos. A lifetime of climbing emotional mountains only to come tumbling down the other side.

I have four Case Studies, a taste of life in the community, interwoven with personal reflections on life. Over ten years working in the community, everything from mental health, drug and alcohol abuse, physical disabilities, domestic and physical abuse. Learning disabilities, the elderly, I encountered every aspects of human life, every age group, every social strata.

I am fairly ambitious; I like to aim for better, better for myself, my clients, my team. My weakness is my inability to leave work at work, to switch off. I suppose like most people, I like to be liked, so I am continually trying to please. This often means I become the 'willing horse,' finding myself frequently drowning in paperwork, meetings and clients. As I work alongside clients, I find their lives are frequently a mirror image of events in my lifetime, maybe others will discover this too.

2 MARCUS

Case Study 1

MARCUS

"The best remedy for those who are afraid, lonely or unhappy is to go outside, somewhere where they can be quiet, alone with the heavens, nature and god. Because only then does one feel that all is as it should be and that God wishes to see people happy, amidst the simple beauty of nature."   Anne Frank

It was one of those days when you wished you could stay in bed for just one more hour. The rain fell in torrents, the windscreen wipers fought frantically to clear the deluge. Steamy windows made visibility poor and spray from the other traffic made progress slow. The Satellite Navigation beeped, and a low female voice said, '*You have now reached your destination.*' I slowed the car and peered through the gloom, the place I wanted was about two hundred feet further along.

I am a Carer, working in the local community. Most people think of care work as low paid, unskilled, work for women. The hours are long with irregular shift patterns, working weekends, evenings and holidays. For the last five years I have worked over the Christmas holidays, not for the money, but to enable my fellow workers with young families to be at home with their children. That's what care workers do, part instinct and part training, we look out for the needs of others. Not that we are saints, I suppose we all have our own reasons and motivations for wanting to be carers. I feel caring is part of my personality, I always classed myself as a people person, wanting to make a difference to people's lives. Even as a child I have memories of caring for others, looking out for the less fortunate, defending the weak and vulnerable. Of course, helping others does give a feeling of satisfaction, making a difference, though sometimes the best laid plans don't always work out and then being a carer can be frustrating, upsetting and de-moralising. I do love my job, although the daily challenges keep me on my toes, driving is one, in rush hour traffic with little or no time between appointments, dashing from one side of town to the next, as today when road conditions are awful. The places we visit are often poorer areas, today I am in an area which is Manchester's equivalent to the Bronx, something of a no- go area for many local people. This year I received two speeding tickets, parking is also a problem, many staff receive local authority parking fines, ironic as we work for the same authority. Then of course the weather, this is Greater Manchester, England, where grey skies and rain are the norm. As Carers we are out in all weather, snow, ice and fog. Sometimes having to trek through snow on foot to reach people in isolated areas. Carers are often the unsung heroes, risking their own safety, to ensure someone gets a visit and a warm meal. The bureaucracy is sometimes unbearable, red tape, form filling, recording of information and endless meetings. Computer literacy and regular training updates pile on the pressure. Sometimes I feel as though actual 'care' is the bottom of the 'to do list'. Yet I still turn up each day, like most carers I enjoy my work, the variety of people we meet, being out in the community not stuck behind a desk, the fact that two days are never the same. Admittedly the job can be stressful, the responsibilities, which without being over dramatic, can often be the difference between life and death. Carers offer a lifeline for many.

Emotionally, dealing with people tugs on the heart strings, no matter how professional or detached you try to be, there is always one person whose story will affect you, touch a nerve bring the tears. Some of my cases are like that, then others bring joy and laughter, a sense of achievement, satisfaction of a job well done, these are the cases I remember if I have a bad day, they boost my spirit and keep me sane.

I manage to park between a skip full of rubble and a beaten-up ford fiesta. my colleague is nowhere in sight, I check my watch, I'm technically five minutes early. Across the street I can see the flat we are to visit, there is no one around. Black plastic rubbish bins line the pavement, their content overflowing onto the street, in the heat of summer the street would smell of rotting food. Most of the buildings to my right are large Victorian, now converted into flats and bedsits. I watch as a young woman emerges from the third floor, carrying a young child and a pushchair down the old iron fire escape. I wonder if she lives here and why, not a place to raise young children. Most of the properties are owned by unscrupulous landlords, who opt for minimum investment and maximum rent. The people living here will cross our paths at some point in their lives, being referred to social services for help and support. This is a place which has lost hope.

There's a sharp knock on the window, I jump and stare at the dark figure. It's Alan, looking very wet, holding on to his collar whilst trying to keep his hood in place. Alan grins. Alan has been coming here for weeks, arriving on the same day, at the same time. Trying to communicate with the client. To date there has been no response, that is why I have been invited along, to see if the client will respond to a female carer. The clients name is Marcus, the last record of any positive feedback was several years ago, when he had a female support worker.

Alan was calm and had lots of patience, he never gave, each week he stayed thirty minutes, crouched down and calling through the letter box, trying to gain a response. Alan started across the street, I followed.

These flats are relatively modern, social housing built in the nineteen sixties, cheaper accommodation for single people. The one window has net curtains, no longer white, folded several times to avoid prying eyes. The small garden to the side of the door has a mountain of discarded cigarette butts. Two small doors sit to the side of the main door, I curiously open the first, it contains a new plastic black wheelie bin, still bearing the delivery sticker, it's empty. The second door is even less interesting, containing an old sweeping brush. The properties belong to a Housing Association, they are the landlords; they are placing pressure on social services to gain access to the property. There are checks which need to be undertaken such as gas safety and electrical maintenance. Marcus, the thirty-five-year-old tenant doesn't answer letters and hasn't spoken with anyone for two years. The one person who knows Marcus is Paul, he works for the mental health team, he is also the liaison officer for the housing association. Paul is going to visit today to see what progress can be made. He is due any minute.

Alan kneels down in front of the letter box, "Hello mate, its Alan, how are you today?" SILENCE.

Alan repeats his question then starts to discuss the weather, to himself, as no one responds. I am cold and damp, slightly apprehensive about the case and what the expectations are; I wish I'd brought a thermos of coffee.

A voice behind me whispers,

"Hi, Carla I presume? Hello Alan, how's it going?

I recognise the soft Irish accent from our telephone call, I have a thing about Irish accents, they mesmerise me. Paul is about six feet tall, dark hair which rests on his collar, penetrating brown eyes and a cheeky, lop sided grin. I like him immediately.

"Any luck?" Paul looks at Alan who shakes his head and starts to stand. Alan is in his sixties now and I can see his arthritis is playing up, he rubs both his knees as he rises.

"How well does Marcus know you?" I ask Paul.

"Oh, I have worked with him for around ten years now, I found this place for him. He's not a big conversationalist as you have probably gathered". Paul took out a pack of cigarettes and offered them to Alan and me. Neither of us smoke, Paul lights his cigarette, continuing with Marcus's information.

"Marcus is a nice guy; he has lots of issues, which is hardly surprising given his family history. He is extremely vulnerable, been in and out of the care system all his life. For fifteen years he lived in various sheltered residential schemes, he became quite institutionalised. Followed the rules but never mixed with anyone, stayed hidden away whenever possible. When he was younger, his fathers died in very upsetting circumstances and Marcus refused to speak for two years, it was like a conscious effort to block out what had happened."

Paul steps over to the letter box,

"Hi Marcus, it's Paul. How you doing mate? Are you going to talk to me today?"

Silence. I feel quite nervous, I have read some of Marcus's file, but details are sketchy, I need to know more. How can I speak to this man if I don't know his history? Paul is still trying to get a response. Paul stands up and Alan prepares to resume his place at the letter box. I wrap my coat tighter attempting to keep out the cold wind, at least the rain has stopped. "So, what actually happened to Marcus?" I look at Paul, he is also starting to feel the cold, pulling his collar up.

"There's not a great deal of information but I will send you what I have. I managed to put a picture together from various reports, Police, Psychiatrist, Marcus also has a Grandmother, though they haven't had contact for over twenty years."

"Is that the only family he has? Alan asks as he struggles to stand, I know him well enough to read the pain on his face. Paul replies as he throws his cigarette butt onto the small pile. I secretly wonder if Paul is solely responsible for the cigarette butt mountain. Paul leans against the wall, he smiles, maybe he is pleased we are so enthusiastic or maybe he's just glad to share the load, he continues,

"Marcus is the youngest of three children. He has an older brother and sister. They live with their mother, somewhere down South, she has never made any attempt to get in touch with

Marcus as far as we know. His Father was a drunk, experimented with drugs, liked to throw his weight around. When Marcus was three years old, she left taking the eldest two with her. Maybe she planned to return for Marcus later? It never happened. Can't say I blame her for leaving, she suffered years of domestic abuse and violence. Physical and mental torture. She was hospitalised nineteen times in a ten-year period, each time the injuries more severe, she refused to press charges. The final time he broke her jaw, two ribs and left her black and blue lying in the street. The police were called, she wouldn't press charges but she did agree the help and she was moved into a woman's hostel in town with the two eldest, Marcus had been taken away on holiday with his grandparents, he remained with them."

Alan's glasses are steamy, he takes out a handkerchief and carefully wipes them. Alan always has a clean handkerchief, he has been happily married for over twenty years, I met Sylvia once. They had a textbook marriage, did everything together, Golf on Saturdays, gardening Sunday, date night every first Friday of the month. Two holidays a year to Portugal, golfing of course. Family round for lunch every second Sunday. Married Bliss? Compared to my life as a widow, on my own for fifteen years, everything had once been great, two healthy children, a happy marriage, except for cancer. One minute you are happy then without warning your life changes completely. Martin died six months after diagnosis. Now the children are independent, I live alone with the cat Mr Tom. Work has become my life, I try not to live for work, but I do have to admit I get a little lonely sometimes and sometimes I even envy Alan's regular, if somewhat boring life.

Paul tries again at the letter box. Silence. Paul indicates for me to have a go, I nervously crouch down, it's not the most comfortable position. My voice breaks a little as I speak,

"Hello Marcus. My name is Carla I work with Alan and Paul. I wonder if there is anything you need. Do you have some cigarettes?" I look at Alan and Paul for reassurance, then peer through the letter box. I can see a figure at the end of the hallway, its dark but I can see he is wearing a coat and a woollen hat. There is an unlit cigarette hanging from his lip.

"Marcus, do you need a light?" I am grasping at straws now. Silence. Then he speaks, quietly,

"Yeah man, yeah." I am so excited he has spoken. I look at Paul, I don't have a light!! Paul grins and passes me a plastic lighter, I push it through the letter box.

"Cheers man, thanks. Will you be here next week?" asks Marcus.

"Yes, yes I will if that's OK with you?" I look into the hallway again, now I can see the faint glow of a cigarette.

"OK man, talk next week." With that Marcus disappears around the corner. I feel ridiculously pleased with myself, maybe I can reach him.

We say our Goodbyes, Paul promises to send me any case information he has before next Wednesday, Alan offers to pick up a sandwich for me on the way back to the office. I smile and sing along to the radio on my way back, it's Al Greene "I'm Tired of being Alone'. How appropriate.

The office is subdued, everyone seems to be in today, which is unusual, maybe it is the weather. It is a great day to catch up on paperwork, though there isn't enough space for everyone. I find a corner to work in, I am reluctant to discuss my new client, its early days. Alan arrives, he throws me a sandwich, wrapped in a brown paper bag, I know he's been to my favourite baker. "Tuna sweetcorn OK?" Alan knows I'm a creature of habit. "Lovely" I smile. I head for the kitchen to grab a coffee, Bill the manager follows me in.

As bosses go, Bill is one of the best, easy going but with twenty years of service under his belt and he knows his stuff. I always found him to be fair and easy to talk to, even if a little absent minded with regards to paperwork. Bill is divorced and now lives with a new partner who also works in the service, I can just imagine their pillow talk!

Bill looks at me, he asks,

"Are you OK? I expect you heard the news, it's very upsetting for everyone." Bill places a hand on my shoulder.

"No, what news is that?" I reach over to the coffee machine, I'm not in the mood to hear the mileage allowance has been cut again or there is a new limit on overtime.

"Oh, didn't you watch the news this morning?" I shake my head disinterestedly.

Bill looks serious,

"There has been an incident. A thirty-two-year-old support worker was killed on duty yesterday in Liverpool. Stabbed to death in a client's home. A forty-year-old man has been charged with murder. Everyone here is really shaken up about it, I have an open-door policy as you know; so if you need to talk about it just come in."

I am stunned, I mumble my words,

"How, did he have a history, were risk assessments in place?" I have so many questions. Bill explains what he knows,

"She has been working with him for six months, no history of violence, some mental health issues. A real tragedy, she was supposed to be getting married next month." Bill squeezes my shoulder as he speaks. I hate to hear things like this, it always unnerves us, we are all aware of our vulnerability out in the community.

"Oh! That's awful, I had no idea. Her poor family, her boyfriend, her friends so many lives affected. It's so sad." I feel like someone I know personally has died.

WHO CARES?

This is an area of the work which scares me. We are sent out into the community, into the unknown, frequently dealing with people who have emotional and mental issues. Our only protection is a mobile phone and a small pocket panic alarm. I did the Defensive Training Module, which I believe would be of absolutely no use in a real-life situation. I was informed how to use the panic alarm, when threatened, open the catch, the alarm will immediately start to sound a high pitch screeching noise. Throw the alarm behind the attacker, when he looks to where the alarm lands. Run. Literally for your life, I am not convinced of this strategy. Usually out alone, often at odd times early morning, late evening, in bad weather. The streets can be scary, you have to be alert. I personally dread one estate, it consists of a number of high rise flats, there are numerous concealed doorways and staircases, at present we have a risk assessment stating two staff must attend all calls on the estate, with gangs lurking on street corners it is scary, even if the entire team of staff were there. Last week a local ambulance was attacked, trying to get help to an elderly man, the gang damaged the ambulance. They stole or damaged equipment and took some needles. The Paramedic and Ambulance personnel were injured, though not life threatening, enough to traumatise them. With all my training, I decided long ago self-preservation instinct is the most important. I try to assess every situation, follow my gut instinct, decide on flight never fight. Misjudging a situation could cost your life. One death is a reality check for us all.

We have a system in the office to keep us 'safe', it's a whiteboard on which we write whenever we leave the building, time we leave, Client we are visiting, expected time of return. Any changes, especially when seeing multiple clients, are supposed to be called in and details amended, that is of course if there's anyone in the office to answer the phone. The theory is someone will notice that you didn't get back when you were supposed to, of course, by this time you could be buried under a patio or taking swimming lessons in the canal.

That evening I call in the supermarket and purchase

three ready meals for one, I can't decide if tonight will be curry or pasta. I spend too long selecting cat food, will Mr Tom really discern between Turkey and Chicken. In terms of selection he has a wider diet than I do. I absently pick up a bottle of red wine, may have a glass tonight instead of Saturday, I am strict about my wine intake, comes of working too long with the Alcohol and Drugs Services. Mr. Tom is on the doorstep waiting, he tries to trip me up on the way to the kitchen, I flick the TV on as I pass through the living room, the sound is comforting. After we've eaten, I switch off the TV, nothing interests me, even the news is all bad. I decide to login and check my emails.

I am quite uplifted to see Paul has written,

Hi Carla, just wanted to say thank you for your help today, it was a real achievement. Hope to see you next week, maybe we could have coffee after to discuss the case? Be lucky.

Marcus file linked attached.

Paul

Coffee? That would be nice, I think. I look at the time the email was sent eight thirty this evening, maybe he is someone like me who finds it hard to switch off? I will reply in the morning. I cannot resist having a preview of the Marcus files though. I pour a glass of wine and press the link. I skim through......

File 677543 Barnes M DOB03.04 1970 Born: Thornton Lancashire

Father Joseph Barnes   Mother Jennifer Haigh

Brother Antony Barnes   Sister Melanie Barnes

Client M first referred to social services in April 1973 when reports of domestic violence were received, at the time the police were called to the family home. Three children were taken into care whilst the mother received hospital treatment.

It is a detailed file, confirming Paul's description,

Marcus had been born into a world of drink, drugs and violence. There were nineteen incidents of domestic abuse detailed, with horrific injuries to the wife, until the final incident when she almost died from injuries. Throughout the abuse she had refused to press charges, then finally she had agreed to accept help and managed to get away. Marcus had spent time with his maternal grandparents and in foster care. Several placements broke down, eventually he went to stay with his paternal grandmother where he achieved a degree of normality for two years, whilst his father served time courtesy of Her Majesty's Prison in Durham.

I close the file, that is enough bedtime reading. I am always amazed by how much violence women tolerate and how prepared to forgive they often are. I remember, last year, I had worked with a client in the local Women's Refuge, I was helping her to find accommodation, get the children in school. Often these women escape the violence with nothing, no money, clothes, belongings. This case had no children involved but had been an horrific case of psychological and physical torture. The Client Sue, was hospitalised for three weeks, placed in an induced coma. She had been so damaged the medical team didn't think she would make it. The partner had been arrested but had an alibi for the night it happened, a 'girlfriend'. When Sue was well enough to be questioned, she refused to press charges. I met her six weeks later in the hostel, she appeared to be doing fine. We started work on finding her a place to live, then looking at her job prospects, her self- esteem and confidence were in shreds, but we managed to chat and raise a few smiles. Then one day she refused to leave the hostel grounds, her ex-partner had been seen in town, Sue was terrified, adamant that she didn't want him anywhere near her. I tried to comfort her, to reassure her, her safety was top priority. Besides her partner was well known to the local police and had been warned not to attempt to go near her. "That won't stop him" she sighed; "He has no fear of the police."

" I can understand your fear after what he did, but I doubt he will be brave enough to hurt you again, he would definitely see a long sentence if he did." Sue stared at me with tears in her eyes and whispered,

"I'm not scared of that; I'm scared that I will go back to him. I still love him."

There was a time when I narrowly missed the same fate, but I didn't want to think about that now. I give Mr. Tom a stroke and we go off to my bed, sleep will be difficult, my mind is still processing all the information. I decide Marcus deserves a better chance at life.

The Second Vis

As I arrive at the flat, I glance at my watch, I'm almost ten minutes late, Alan likes to be on time. I see Alan bending down at the letter box. I rush across and offer my apologies. Alan doesn't seem bothered; he just waves for me to have a go at the letter box.

"Hello, Marcus its Carla again. How are you today?" Silence. I feel disappointed. I decide to try again,

"Marcus, will you be watching the match tonight? I am a City fan who do you support?" Silence. Then,

"They are rubbish man, United will win. Yeah I watch it on BBC". Marcus speaks quietly with a slight accent. I know I need to keep up the banter, but my football knowledge is limited. I look to Alan for help, Alan whispers in my ear and I pass on the message,

"City only need to win this game and they are in the premiership. Alan here supports United; he thinks United will win."

Marcus replies almost instantaneous,

"City won't win. Good man Alan, knows which is the best team".

Alan bends down and there is soon a flow of football conversation between the two men, through the letter box. I listen feeling quite smug. A hand touches my shoulder, Paul is all smiles as he realises, we have a breakthrough, if only a small one. I ask Paul how Marcus shops, if he doesn't go out. Paul gives me a cheeky grin and explains,

"Marcus is a night owl; he never goes out before the sun goes down. He shops at the local corner store; he walks there in the shadows, so no one sees him. He buys mostly ready-made meals for one, cigarettes and lager. I don't think his diet is particularly well balanced"

Not unlike my diet I smile to myself, except of course for the cigarettes and lager.

"Did you read the file?" Paul asks. I haven't had chance to study the whole file, its several pages long and written mainly in social service jargon. I decide to just nod.

I did know the important pieces of information. I knew Marcus had slipped out of Social Service's radar on several occasions, his father had frequently handed the care of Marcus to his own mother, Marcus's grandparents had taken responsibility for him, given him a secure home, schooling and a relatively safe home. Joe, his father, spent months in prison, charges of Grievous Bodily Harm, Drug Dealing and a charge of domestic violence, apparently his new partner wasn't as understanding and forgiving as his wife. Joe was an evil piece of work, the Judge who tried him said he was particularly concerned about the sheer aggression Joe had demonstrated, beating up a man over a drugs deal, Joe had continued kicking and punching the man long after the man had lost consciousness. Joe's parents helped him when he got out of prison, I always wonder how far family loyalty will stretch, what crimes are hidden because an offender is 'family'.

Marcus spent time with Joe and soon he was skipping school and mixing with some unsavoury characters. Joe took Marcus to live with him, the grandparents didn't report this, so for months Marcus was not registered as a child at risk. Joe moved them to Leeds, then after a couple of years back to Manchester. Joe was now back to his dealing, only now he'd progressed to cocaine, LSD and his old stand- by cannabis. Marcus had learned to be a 'runner' delivering drugs to regular clients on the estate, he witnessed some scary stuff, from the age of eleven he was in regular company of users and dealers, he was also part of the street gangs, violence and crime were part of his daily life. Grandparent's intervention had ceased, they moved away, Grandfather passed away shortly after.

Alan stood up and indicated for Paul to speak,

"Hi Marcus, Paul here. Listen mate I have an idea, I was wondering how you would feel about having a mobile phone?" At first there was no response, Marcus was considering the information,

"Yeah man, but I don't have anyone to ring".

I bend down and balance on my heels, I can see Marcus,

"Hi Marcus. It would be great if we could use the phone to keep in touch, to let you know when we are coming, you could ring us too if you need anything." Marcus was silent, two, three minutes pass then answers "OK" as he disappears out of sight. End of communications for today.

"Coffee?" Paul asks looking at me, "Yeah, sounds good". Alan replies before I have chance. Ten minutes later we are sat in the local coffee shop drinking and Alan has treated us to fruit scones. I am aware that scones are the last thing I should be eating, not that I count calories, but my sweet tooth is piling on an extra tyre. When I was younger I didn't worry, now it was much harder to get rid of. I remember sitting on the bed one morning in my bra and pants, Martin looked at me and, in all seriousness said, "You should have been a magician", Such a random comment, "Why?" I asked, "Because you make your panties disappear just by sitting up". Though I did laugh at the time, I went on a diet the next day.

Alan finishes first, he leans over and stirs his coffee. I bet Sylvia does not allow scones or coffee, I think to myself. Alan asks,

"So, what is the formal medical diagnosis for Marcus?" His question is directed at both of us, I haven't read that far yet, so I look to Paul for a reply.

"Marcus was in our supported residential unit for ten years, he followed the rules but struggled with people, rarely left his room, never made any friends. The unit was due to be closed due to lack of funding, so I needed to find Marcus somewhere quick. The flat he's in now became available, to qualify for it I needed to obtain an up-to-date assessment of his health, physical and mental. We were able to register him with a GP some years ago, though he had never visited. After a lot of effort, we got the GP to come and do the assessment at the shelter. He gave Marcus a clean bill of health, though he did question his personal hygiene. A Psychiatrist was appointed, unfortunately there was a six-month waiting list. Marcus was allowed to move in subject to the receipt of a satisfactory psychiatric report. The said appointed psychiatrist made three visits to the flat and then wrote her assessment, based upon his file history and his non-communication through the letter box."

We both looked at Paul in disbelief, Paul smirked at the ridiculous nature of the assessment.

"Marcus has been formally diagnosed with PTSD (Post Traumatic Stress Disorder). Anxiety, mostly likely based upon Marcus's replies to constant questions, through the letter box, which were to tell Psychiatrist to "Go away" in far more explicit terms. Finally, OCD (Obsessive Compulsive Disorder) based largely on the information we provided from his behaviour in the home, we had to gain access to his room every four weeks to remove garbage on Health and Safety grounds. He was pretty good about it, though staff hated the job. He still requires support with this and also managing his allowance. His rent and

29

household bills are managed by our staff, I'm kind of hoping your department will eventually take over this".

I have researched PTSD to discover it is often related to severe traumatic events, often events which threaten the persons life. Soldiers frequently suffer, particularly after active service in war zones. People with PTSD often experience high anxiety, nightmares, flashbacks and some have physical pain. Anxiety in itself is a common condition, OCD is another type, worry and fear are constant and overwhelming for the individual, often OCD includes repetitive behaviour, always checking windows, doors, hoarding, switching electrical appliances off, rechecking several times. Like most mental health disorders there are degrees of severity, no two people are exactly the same. The strangest example I ever came across was a man who could not walk across squares, including tiled floors and paved walkways. He told me he had to plan any journeys around the floor covering. Often to get from A to B required an excursion, around non-square routes, sometimes taking him miles away from where he wanted to be.

We finish our coffee and say our Goodbyes, agreeing to meet up same place, same time next week. Paul mentions he is getting lots of pressure from above. We need to speak with Marcus about access to the flat next visit.

By one o'clock I am ready for lunch, somehow the cheese and tomato sandwich, prepared at seven this morning does not look tempting. Especially as Alan had just returned to the office, with a flask of home-made chicken soup, which smells delicious. Note to self I think, make some soup!

The door to the office crashes open and all eyes are propelled away from the computer screens to the source, there is Lacey, the new Social Worker. Not a small lady by any stretch of the imagination. Her flowing ankle length skirt, wafts around cleaning any dust from the office floor, and serves to enhance her bulk. Today her skirt is floral, last week it was black arrayed with stars and moons. Alan had then quietly whispered to me, "look out Merlin has just arrived." Now I cannot shake that image from my mind. Lacey's face is a perfect reflection of her diet. Rounded and golden, with peach coloured cheeks and cherry lips. Her hair is like strands of candy floss, piled high with no particular style. Under one arm she carries a box, a large Blueberry Muffin with a bite missing is sitting in her hand. Over her shoulder hangs a large satchel overflowing with files and paper. Lacey always looks busy, yet she always has time for a chat and a snack. She places the box on the table and pushes it towards me. More Blueberry Muffins, seven to be precise.

"Help yourselves, I cannot eat any more, this is my third."

Alan, Mike and Shirley dive into the box. I show great restraint, remembering the scone from earlier. Lacey lowers herself slowly onto the seat opposite mine, it is the only computer available. We call this practise 'hot desking' which means if you are lucky you can find somewhere to sit, if you are super lucky there is a computer free too. Lacey tips the contents of her bag on to the desk, pushing what is left of her muffin into her mouth. As she sorts through the files, her right hand subconsciously seeks out the box of muffins, before she realises it, she is halfway through another muffin. Licking her fingers, she turns to address the entire office,

"Has anyone seen Pete G this week?" several crumbs escaped onto the floor. Various heads around the office shake and some reply "No" without looking up.

"Damn, he is never at home and does not answer his phone. His weight is becoming a real issue. I need to talk to him about his diet, he is eating all the wrong things and doesn't know when to stop."

I almost choke on my coffee, the Queen of Muffins worried about diets? We are all aware that Pete suffers from Prada-Willi Syndrome, which has several physical affects on a sufferer, poor growth, delayed development, temper tantrums, to name but a few. Among the conditions is compulsive behaviour, in Pete's

31

case compulsive eating. I wonder if other people suffer with this, whilst remaining blissfully unaware.

The afternoon passes quickly, the mood is good. I have two routine visits after which I hope to finish early. We operate a flexitime policy at the moment, whereby its possible to start an hour early, regaining the hour at the end of the day. My visits go well and by four o'clock I'm on route home. Home to another meal for one and as its Tuesday, an evening in the company of a friend, who likes to unburden her unhappy marriage, to a 'Twitcher' who frequently disappears looking for birds, of the feathered variety?

The Third Visit.

Although its still grey the rain has stopped, I park opposite the flat. Paul is already there. He waves. Alan won't be here this morning he has car trouble at home, so he is going to the garage first. As Paul is attending it isn't essential for Alan to be present. The risk assessment states two members of staff at all visits, of course, this is assuming we will ever actually enter the premises.

Paul stands up from the letter box shaking his head and proffering for me to have a go.

"Hi Marcus, its Carla here. How are you today?" Silence. "Marcus we would like to talk to you about your flat, would that be OK?" Silence. I fumble my words and wonder if I should have mentioned the flat. Paul shows me a mobile phone, he is adding numbers to the contact list. I change my subject,

"Marcus, Paul has got a mobile phone for you here. Do you know how to use one?"

"Yeah man of course". Marcus replies indignantly. What a stupid question, of course he knows how to use one I chastise myself.

"Great, that's great. I am going to post it through the letter box now. Its all set up ready to go. We have put our numbers in so that you can call us anytime". Another stupid statement, the last thing any of us needs is random calls in the middle of the night. I push the phone and charger through the letter box. Another silly question leaves my lips,

"If you prefer you can text message us. Do you know how to text?"

"Yeah man, yeah." Marcus replies impatiently.

I stare through the letter box, Marcus is examining the phone, there's another unlit cigarette hanging from his lip and his woollen hat is pulled down over his eyebrows. He looks like an oversized child examining his first toy, he's tall and quite stocky in build. I can make out basic features, he is a good-looking young man, his skin is dark and I suspect his eyes will be brown.

"Paul, you got a light mate?" Paul stepped forward and pushed a small lighter through the letter box, a few seconds later the lighter comes back.

I watched as Marcus turns and slowly shuffles down the hallway. This is going to be the end of communications for the day.

"Marcus, is it OK to talk about the flat? We need to come in soon, can we talk". Silence.

I stand up, both legs are numb, Paul grins and gives me a thumbs up. "Well, I think that deserves a coffee, same place?" I nod, I had been secretly hoping for a chance to talk to him, so much I wanted to know.

        The coffee meeting is going well, Paul is easy to talk to he is obviously fully committed to his job which meant most of our conversation is work related. I ask Paul how Marcus buys clothes or goes shopping for things other than food. Paul says to the best of his knowledge Marcus has worn the same clothes for over two years. Paul is not even sure Marcus ever takes them off, or if he washes. One thing he emphasises is the need to gain access to the flat is critical.

Paul does mention that he is single, he has had a long-term relationship but that ended two years ago. He lives alone with his dog, a black Labrador, something we talk about for a while, I have had Labradors in the past and particularly love the breed. He also lives about two miles away from me. After coffee Paul says he looks forward to next week and coffee.

As I drive home that evening, I review my day and go through my plans for the following day. Tomorrow is my monthly supervision with Bill, I need to have my caseload reports up to date. I quite enjoy the supervision meetings, it is an opportunity to unload any concerns, to discuss each case, to exchange ideas and to get feedback on my own performance, everyone likes to hear guidance and a little praise. I will read the rest of Marcus's file this evening.

Later, having shared my pasta with Mr Tom, I settle down to finish reading the rest of Marcus's file.

By age eleven Marcus had a life not dissimilar to the Artful Dodger in Oliver Twist, instead of pickpocketing, he was delivering and collecting payment for drugs. He knew his way around the estate, knew who lived where, which houses were being watched by the police. He also knew which users were desperate for the drugs, so he added on a small delivery charge which over the course of a week gave him a nice little income. Marcus knew the main dealers, the Street Gangs, who to avoid, who to pay off. Marcus dealt with the low life of the town, he witnessed first hand the effects of 'Class A' drugs on users, although he was exposed to all this, there was never any evidence that he was using, he turned up for school two or three times a week. Social Services spoke to his father on numerous occasions without any positive outcome, threats were made about care, fines, imprisonment. Marcus would conform for a few weeks then he would take time out. The schools found him difficult to manage, he was a loner and didn't follow rules.

We tend to underestimate a child's ability to understand and cope with life. Marcus's childhood had some similarities to my own, I spent the first eight years of my life on an estate full of characters. The housing estate was my territory, I knew my way around, I could travel from one end to the other without ever being seen. I knew who lived where, how many children they had, who was in prison and usually I knew what they were in prison for, children are a great source of information. I knew who was in trouble for fighting, drugs, not paying their bills or being cruel to their dog. I knew the dynamics of the families, number of children, other relatives, divorced or who had two dads. Whether parents were strict, kind, friendly or mean. A child knows when secrets need to be kept. I saw my friends mother kiss a neighbour's husband; I never spoke about it. I knew one girl's uncle had frequently touched her where he shouldn't, I was sworn to secrecy. I ignored the oath and told the girls mother. There followed a terrible fight and the uncle was taken away. I saw the older boys buying and selling cigarettes, they chased me away. I suspected the cigarettes were stolen. I never told; those boys were mean I didn't want to get hurt. Maybe this is where my interest in people first began, I witnessed the poverty, crime and the injustice of life. Where some lives were easy and others hard.

Eventually Joe got out of his depth, no longer dealing with the twenty pound a week orders, he started to meet the more profitable dealers. They were moving an entire supermarket range of drugs on to the estate for re-distribution through the town. It appears Joe got a bit greedy. A package of Heroin, said to be worth around twenty thousand pounds went missing. It was set for delivery from the head man to the main distributor, known on the estate as the Smithy, a real hard man, criminal record for armed robbery and other violence. Joe was asked to deliver a package to the Smithy, Joe said he had Marcus deliver the drugs. The package went missing. Joe said Marcus had it, Marcus said he passed it to the Smithy and the Smithy claimed he never got delivery. A gang war broke out, everyone was blaming each other, no one really knew, there were three stabbings and one shooting linked to the missing heroin. Joe took Marcus and left in the night. Marcus and Joe were the last people to see the heroin. They went to Wales where they stayed in a caravan. They were hidden for around three months, then one evening three thugs turned up at the caravan. They had lost their heroin and were not leaving until they discovered where it was. They started with Joe, torture, slowly and methodically. They broke all his fingers until Joe passed out with the pain. They then turned to Marcus, who was terrified and cowering in the corner. It was going to be a long few hours, they first tried cigarette burns, they stripped him naked and continued burning him. Two of them sexually assaulted him, he tried to fight back but he was no match. They then took a knife to him, just deep enough to scar. Marcus howling like an animal raised the alarm, an elderly couple phoned the police. The caravan was wrecked, blood everywhere, Joe awake now, watched as the thugs cut and burned Marcus, who was just fifteen years old. When the police sirens were heard the thugs ran, before they left, they gave Joe a parting gift, they slit his throat. Joe was dead by the time the ambulance arrived. Marcus was taken to hospital; he was bleeding heavily and in shock. At the inquest for Joe they said Marcus had over thirty cigarette burns on his body, ten of which were historical, possibly three to four years old. He also had ten lacerations covering his body, a deeper laceration requiring ten stitches above his genital area. There were also signs of anal penetration with bruising and broken skin. The thugs set out to scar Marcus physically and mentally, they certainly achieved that. He spent a month in hospital and two years without speaking. He then had another fourteen years in institutional care for the mentally ill.

I close the file; this is the worst case of abuse I have ever worked with. I go into the kitchen and pour myself a stiff drink, gin and tonic is all that I have. I could not even begin to comprehend this man's life, his suffering, his pain. I go upstairs, get undressed and climb into the shower; the tears fall easily in the gushing water. I feel so sad and overwhelmed by the complexity and emotion this case invokes.

I look at the clock, three am. I remember being fifteen, I knew of a drug culture. I became involved, most of the people were male, most were older than me. I only ever tried the light drug cannabis, convinced that anything else would leave me addicted. There were around twenty boys involved with the drugs, during that year three died from drug and alcohol poisoning. Someone explained to me that the alcohol made them sick and the drugs caused them to choke and die. I had no idea if this was true, but it certainly sounded an horrific death. My mentor in this world was a boy, he was three years older, my first love I told myself. After a few weeks of convincing myself that this was true love and I could change him, he attacked me in the street. He pulled me by my hair, threw me down a flight of steps and kicked me as I lay on the floor. He only stopped the attack when two men arrived, he ran. I hate thinking about this, hate the fact that I believed I still loved him, that he still loved me. The police refused to take any action, saying in effect by being in a 'relationship' I had brought this about. No thoughts about age, no thoughts of assault. It was a hard lesson for me. The cuts and bruises healed but my confidence, pride, my broken heart would take years to heal, trust and love became difficult. I never really spoke about my feelings, just locked them away in a compartment of my mind where I didn't have to visit them. Marcus would have these external and internal scars for life, his were far deeper reaching than mine, far more painful. It was going to be a long difficult road back for Marcus. I say a little prayer for him before I attempt sleep again.

The Fourth Visit

Its not been a good week, my washing machine decided to stop working, my son's car failed its road worthiness test, needing at least five hundred pounds worth of repairs. On top of that it was trying to snow. I had a little money put buy for a holiday, now it seemed I would need it for more urgent issues. Both my children are independent, they very rarely ask for help, being a single parent, I find it hard to help out financially. I sometimes envy people who plan for the future, I always live for the day. When discussing money my father used to say, 'no matter how bad things get you will never hit rock bottom.' His other words of wisdom, 'However successful you become in life, never forget your roots'. I suppose in his eyes I had been successful, twenty years ago I had a very successful career, climbing the corporate ladder in five years to a senior managerial role. We owned a large Victorian semi in the South of England, had two cars, two holidays abroad a year and a very comfortable lifestyle. When I look back now it seems like someone else lived that life. Now I live in a small two up two down terrace, in a suburb of Greater Manchester, I own a five year old Corsa. After several years of ill health, I finally managed to secure this post as a Carer, with a salary just above the minimum hourly rate.

I park the car opposite the flat and I am surprised to see the front door wide open. Grabbing my coat and bag I walk across to see a man carrying two black sacks of rubbish and stacking them against several other bags on the pavement. As I approach, he wipes both his hands on his jeans and offers a handshake,

"Good morning, you must be Carla. I'm Steve, I work with Paul."

"What's going on?" I ask, wondering if something has happened to Marcus.

"Oh, it was decided yesterday afternoon that we would clear the flat of rubbish today. The other services want to get in on Friday. Paul's inside, it is a state in here. We have organised a skip for one o'clock, so we need to get the bulk of rubbish out before then.

"So where is Marcus? Is he OK?" I ask. Something like this is a major issue for people like Marcus, his anxiety levels I know will be through the roof.

"He's not happy, supposed to be helping Paul in the bedroom." Steve turned back into the flat and I followed.

Inside is like the twilight zone, Marcus has lived here for two years, during which time he has never opened a window, or thrown anything away. There is a small sitting room, it looks like a sepia photograph, everything is coated in a thick film of brown nicotine. The window is roughly boarded over by what appears to be an old pallet, the boards are on the inside. There are small slithers of light breaking through the boards, the curtains hang limply at each side. I look around trying not to breathe in too deeply, the smell is overwhelming, a mixture of tobacco, food waste, urine and another, which I cannot identify but it could be something has died. There is a stark forty-watt bulb hanging from the ceiling, in one corner of the room a large TV set is on with the sound very low, its odd to see the Breakfast time presenters smiling and laughing, in this surreal environment. On the other side of the room Rock music pours out from a small stereo, just loud enough to drown out the TV. In the centre is a sofa, covered by a not too clean quilt, an old pillow in the corner, this is obviously were he sleeps. In front of the sofa there's a small table, filled with empty lager cans; two large bar ashtrays are overflowing with dead cigarette ends. The walls are covered in wallpaper which I suspect is brightly coloured underneath the nicotine glaze. The carpet no longer has a colour or a pattern, just years of grime trodden solid into the fibres. I hear raised voices in the other room and Paul emerges carrying three rubbish bags.

"Ho, Hi Carla, glad you are here, I don't suppose you could make a start on the kitchen, it's filthy. I reckon we will fill another fifty of these bags before we are done!" Paul gives me a wink as he disappears out the door. I gaze into the kitchen, he isn't joking, I wonder where on earth I will start. Then I hear raised voices again, this time they are shouting and angry, it's Steve,

"Marcus this is disgusting, did you do this? Its stinks, why have you got pee all over your bed? The mattress is completely ruined, it's got to be thrown. Oh man I never saw such filth", Steve voice is exasperated.

"Leave it man, leave it. I'll sort it just leave it. It weren't me man". Marcus is more sad than angry.

I decide to go in, Marcus is standing in the corner staring at the floor, he looks lost and upset. I approach him,

"Hi Marcus, it's Carla, would you like to come in the kitchen with me and I'll make you a cup of tea. Maybe you can tell me how you are today?" Marcus avoids eye contact and remains silent. I go back into the kitchen. I locate the kettle and some mugs, they are dirty, every plate cup, pan has been used, dirty pots are stacked high on every flat surface. I find the washing up liquid, its old, original packaging, it was probably in the flat when he moved in. I wash some mugs. As I start to search for more mugs Marcus comes in. He has the familiar cigarette hanging from his lip. It's the first time I have seen him close up, he looks so young, he has brown oval eyes, he is very good looking. Under different circumstances he would have been extremely popular with the young girls. He gives me a half smile and his face lights up, his teeth are white. If he doesn't wash or shower there is no evidence, his face looks clean, he has shaved. I am unable to see his hair, hidden under the woollen hat. His clothes do look shabby, he has a pair of jogging pants on, it is difficult to tell their colour, a black quilted jacket with a tear on the sleeve and several stains down the front. The soles of his trainer's flap, not so much talking but shouting at him.

"Are you alright Marcus? I am so sorry about this." I watch for a reaction, he nods slowly,

"They shouldn't touch my stuff, they came in with a key, this is my flat, my space. No way man, they need to leave me alone".

WHO CARES?

Marcus looks anxious and hurt.

"I'm so sorry it happened this way Marcus, we are trying to help you. We want you to be able to continue living here. To do that we must get some people in to check the gas and electric. Do you understand?" I wasn't sure if he understood. He stared at the floor,

"This is my place, my stuff they shouldn't touch it." I could see Marcus was physically shaking as he spoke.

"I'm sorry. Can I make you a cup of tea, or coffee? It will be all over in a little while and we will leave you in peace. Come on have a brew with me". I give him my warmest smile and sorted out four mugs, I'm not sure if I can face drinking anything here. Ten minutes later we are stood drinking coffee in the kitchen, Paul and Steve have theirs in the living room. Marcus seems a little calmer.

"Sorry for swearing earlier, I just got so mad with them. It's not right is it? How would they like me to just go into their houses, go through their stuff, I bet they'd call the cops?" I hadn't heard him swearing, I suppose this had happened when Paul and Steve first arrived.

I nod agreement, I don't really know what to say, I don't agree with how this has been done, they could have done more harm than good. Something like this could trigger panic attacks, anxiety; Marcus could close up completely. Our violation of his home, his property, his privacy is devastating and traumatic for him. Marcus stays in the kitchen with me, he asks if I have a house, if I have children. Sometimes I feel its good to share a little bit about yourself, nothing too personal but enough to make you real. Marcus is interested that I have children, I tell him their ages and where they are working. I also tell him about Mr. Tom and some of the antics he gets up to. Marcus laughs, he says he used to have a cat a long time ago called Charcoal, because he lived in the coal cellar. Marcus smiles as he describes sneaking the cat into his bedroom and being in trouble the next day for

41

getting the bed dirty. I continue cleaning as we talk, Marcus seems relaxed eager to chat. The kitchen is starting to look cleaner, all the pots are washed and stacked away, the cooker however will need a lot more work, I have to be back in the office so I doubt the cooker will be cleaned today, if ever.

Steve comes into the kitchen, I watch Marcus flinch and cast his eyes down, he's clearly not comfortable with Steve.

"Right mate, the mattress has been thrown away but hopefully we can get a new one in by tomorrow, Paul will come and meet the delivery men. No peeing on the new one though mate, that's totally unacceptable." Steve looked at me shaking his head. Marcus spoke in a low voice,

"It weren't me". Steve through his arms up in the air and is shaking his head as he leaves. I watch Marcus,

"I believe you, but who did it Marcus? You shouldn't let people like that in." I try to sound reasonable, Marcus nods and gives a half smile then asks, "You got a light." and I wonder if he's telling the truth. There is obviously more to Marcus than I first realised, there is definitely something he isn't telling us.

As lunchtime approaches, we decide to call it a day, there are over fifty bags of rubbish for the skip, including three bags of used toilet paper. Three sacks of empty lager cans; the rest general domestic garbage. We say our goodbyes, Marcus looks sad, like a child who had just lost hope. We have taken away everything familiar, the rubbish, litter, the smells and rotting food waste. The indistinguishable smell is a dead rat, which Paul removes from behind the sofa. We agree to leave the window boarded up. Our sense of achievement is Marcus's sense of trespass and intrusion. Marcus is standing in the hallway, his unlit cigarette hanging from his mouth, this is someone's son, lonely, confused and vulnerable. I give him a gentle wave and whisper, "See you next week, message me if you need anything." I really feel like giving him a hug, to reassure him, but that is unprofessional.

WHO CARES?

Back at the office I cannot face the thought of food, the images of bacon fat and grease coating the cooker turn my stomach. I can still smell the flat on my clothes, I can't wait till I get home for a hot shower.

Later that evening Marcus is still in my thoughts, imagine if he lived next door, would I help him? Would I even know about him? Care in the Community they call it, large asylums of the nineteenth century, all but gone, people who are different now live in the community. Or maybe they always have; we just haven't noticed. I remember my childhood, my Grandma, always giving advice, "Now don't you go near number thirty-six, there is a bad man living there". She made me promise, of course, I had my fingers crossed behind my back. I passed the house of the 'bad man' every day, I never saw him, I was beginning to think he didn't exist. Then one day I persuaded a friend to come to the house with me. We knocked on the door, to our surprise it opened and there stood a short, bald man with round spectacles, he smiled at us and asked,

"Yes, how can I help you two young ladies". My friend glanced at me, I improvised,

"Erm, we wondered if you needed anything from the shop, we could fetch it for you". He again smiled and thanked us but said he didn't need anything. As we started to leave, he asked, "Do you like Guinea Pigs?" we both nodded. "Would you like to come and see mine?" We looked at each other then both nodded in unison. Inside we were amazed, it was a living room like no other. All four walls were lined floor to ceiling with cages, in the centre was a chair, a small table and a TV. The cages contained Guinea Pigs of all sizes and colours, for two young girls this was wonderful. He immediately lifted out different ones, told us the names of them, allowing us to hold and stroke them, we were fascinated as he explained what they ate, how long they lived and how many babies they could have. After a while my guilty conscience kicked in, we made our excuses and left, he told us we could go back anytime. I suppose as an adult his behaviour was

43

odd but to a young child, he was gentle and kind. I knew he wasn't a bad man; my Grandma took a different view, especially when I accidentally mentioned the visit, I never went back to visit the guinea pigs, I didn't dare.

The Fifth Visit

Alan and I arrive at the same time, we talk to the letter box for twenty minutes, nothing just silence. We take turns, try different subjects. It appears Marcus is not going to communicate. My concern for Marcus grew, what if we had pushed him too far? Don't take the work home, that was the general golden rule, far easier said than done, I could not switch off my subconscious. I decided I would text message Marcus the next day.

The Sixth Visit

Last week I was very surprised to have a text back from Marcus. It said, 'Sorry missed you. Was seeing my Grandma. See you next week.' This in itself was a breakthrough, now he was messaging and agreeing to meet. I needed to do some quick research about his Grandma, I didn't think they had any contact. I rang Paul, Paul was surprised, he knew that Marcus had her address but wasn't aware there had been any contact. Marcus had visited twice but never actually gone in, he had been reported to the police for loitering, they had warned him to keep away. Paul didn't think they had made contact but suggested I call Elsie, Marcus's Grandma. Elsie sounded lovely, yes, she had seen Marcus last week, she had waved to him but he went away without actually speaking to her. She would very much like to see him. Elsie became quite emotional on the telephone, she had lost her son Joe, her two grandchildren and then Marcus, her husband had also died five years ago. She was confined to a wheelchair and would do anything to see Marcus and talk. I promised to see what I could do.

Alan and I decided to car share this visit, his car as he doesn't like my driving, he complains I drive too fast. Upon arriving the front door is ajar, I push it and call in. No reply, we both step into the hallway, announcing our arrival, Marcus comes into the hall, smiling and waving the sports page. Marcus is something of an expert on sports, football, rugby, tennis and snooker, he is a TV player. His knowledge is amazing; Alan jokes that we have to take him to a Pub Quiz because he would win the sports round. Turns out, he would probably win the Geography, History and Music round too. Years of TV had not been wasted, he watched the news daily so was informed about current affairs, he enjoyed documentaries and for someone who had never travelled further than Leeds, he certainly knew his way around maps. After an hour of chatter, or to be more precise interesting conversation, Marcus says,

"You are busy people I think you need to go now". That was our cue, I am impressed that Marcus had talked with us for an hour; and more impressed that he never removed the unlit cigarette from his mouth.

"Oh Marcus, just one thing. I spoke with your Grandma Elsie, she would like you to go and visit with me, I thought maybe next week?" I watch his expression turn to panic, "No, no not possible." He started to shuffle away.

"OK, at least think about, I will take you in my car. Text me." I call out, unaware if he hears me.

The Tenth Visit

The previous visits have been great, every week we get to know Marcus a little better. He doesn't talk about the past, just odd references here or there. He is really growing more confident in our company. He has recently texted jokes to both Alan and I, some didn't have a punchline, some I just didn't get. Alan usually had a football joke to text back. This visit was extra special because Marcus had texted that he wants to see his Grandmother. I have contacted Elsie and we are going for coffee at ten this morning. When I arrive, Marcus is waiting in the street, he climbs into the car and seems suitable impressed with the Corsa,

"I could drive one of these, well if I had a license". He grins and starts to look through my music collection. He is pleased to see my Motown collection and he too is a fan of John Lennon, though he's disappointed I have no serious Rock music.

We arrive at Elsie's bungalow to Michael Jackson singing 'Man in the Mirror' at full volume, I quickly turn it down. Marcus is now very quiet, he is reluctant to leave the car, I coax him out of the car and to the door. I ring the bell, even though the door is ajar.

"Come in Marcus, I saw you both arrive". Elsie sounds very happy. Marcus looks like a rabbit trapped in the headlights; I have to virtually drag him through the door. The living room is small warm and inviting, family photos and souvenirs from a lifetime adorn every shelf. Elsie is just how I imagine her, soft round cheery face, with a welcoming smile, a hint of mischief, grey hair permed in the traditional short style. She looks at Marcus and her eyes fill,

"Marcus, come here, let your Grandma see you, its been a long time, too long." As she speaks tears roll down her face and she fishes a tissue from her pocket.

"I should have done more, come here, have you got a hug for your old Grandma?" Marcus surprises us both by walking and bending over to hug Elsie, a little awkward but a hug, nevertheless. Elsie wipes more tears away, she is laughing and sobbing at the same time,

"Look at me, I'm so pleased to see you. I have lots of questions. How tall are you, do you have curly hair like your Granddad? "

Elsie hardly draws a breath as the questions continue to pour out. Marcus struggles to answer. "Do you like where you live? Do you still read? Do you have a girlfriend?" Marcus smiles at the last question and I wonder if he has ever had a girlfriend. Elsie then offers us a cup of coffee; I volunteer to make it so they can chat. I produce a pack of chocolate digestives I picked up this morning. I'm ridiculously happy to hear the two generations talking, Marcus asks his own questions. "What happened to Granddad? How long have you lived here? Do you still go to the Squirrel park? We drink the coffee and Marcus eats half of the biscuits,

"Forgot my breakfast". He smiles. After a while Marcus looks at me, I know what's coming, he's ready to leave. We say our Goodbyes with a promise that another visit will take place very soon, Marcus nods at this suggestion. The journey back is quieter, the Beatles lull us along, Marcus looks relaxed and somehow different, more, more 'loved'. As he gets out of the car Marcus turns and says,

"Elsie's a good person, isn't she?" He didn't need a reply as he turned and walked to his flat.

As I drive back to the office, I remember my Grandparents, they had played a vital role in my early years, they were virtual parents to me whilst my parents worked. All my early memories are of them, no expensive toys, no fancy holidays but they had one thing most parents lack, time. Time to play games, read stories, go for walks, teach me baking, to sing, to draw and to use imagination. It must have been hard for Elsie to watch Joe in the life he chose and what he did to his wife and children. I was fortunate, my parents were good, honest hard working people. Yet at eight years old I still felt a wrench of separation, when we

47

moved to a new house; I could no longer pay daily visits to my grandparents. Marcus has to deal with feelings of abandonment; being unloved and unwanted has emotionally scarred him.

Back at the office Bill is waiting by my desk, I remember, he changed my supervision to this afternoon, Great I had some really positive stuff to share. In the service we always try to promote family involvement in cases, Marcus and his Grandmother are a good example.

"Two minutes, I'll just get my papers I wink at Bill, he tuts and goes to his office. I'm only fifteen minutes late, he's usually much later.

The Thirteenth Visit

Alan has been absent all week, some form of 'man flu' so I have been covering some of his cases. Yesterday I took Kathy G for her Medical Examination into the centre of Manchester. These examinations are routine for anyone in receipt of Incapacity Benefit, from the Department of Social Security. Reviews are currently set annually or three yearly. These are to 'confirm' the incapacity is still applicable. In the case of Kathy G it is somewhat superfluous. Kathy has a Learning Disability, from birth. Kathy's speech is affected, she stammers to such a degree, particularly when upset or stressed, she is incomprehensible. Kathy does not read or write, and has difficulty following basic instructions. Kathy is stunning, her looks would be the envy of most professional models, six feet tall, (mostly leg) thick flowing natural blonde hair and a figure with all the curves in the right places. All of which means Kathy, at twenty, is extremely vulnerable. Kathy gave birth to a son three months ago and lives with her baby in a women's hostel, where she is learning to care for the baby. The father of the baby is currently serving eight years for Burglary and assault.

We arrive at the building, it's in the centre, parking is

difficult, the building is concealed behind various other high-rise offices. I can feel the tension growing in Kathy. We are given a form by reception, which I dutifully complete on Kathy's behalf, Kathy's stammer has increased, I obtain a tea for her from the machine, in an attempt to relax her. We are then called in. The 'doctor' looks old and ill and I wonder why he is still working. He has Kathy's file, he starts to ask Kathy questions,

"How are you today?" he looks first to Kathy then to me. Kathy speaks, even I am unsure of her answer. He tries again with several other questions,

"How old are you? Where do you live? You have a baby?" Kathy mumbles and stutters, none of her answers are understandable. I have been instructed not to intervene until asked to. I stare at him, the hairs in his ears are long, he has the hairiest ears I've ever seen, I stop myself from laughing out loud. He then asks,

"So how long have you had this learning disability Kathy?" I cannot not believe the question, he has her file, he has her history, what is he trying to prove. He continues,

"Do you have any problems with your health, any aches and pains?" Kathy stares at me then shakes her head.

"Well, give this paper to the receptionist on the way out. And ask her to send the next person in." The end of the interview, no time wasted on pleasantries such as Good morning or Goodbye.

We forget to send his next victim in. Kathy is visibly distressed when we get into the car. I put the CD player on and asked her to pick a tune. Ten minutes later Kathy is singing at the top of her voice, not a stammer to be heard, she knew every word of the song. When we arrive back at the hostel Kathy smiles and word perfect says,

"Thanks, I'm worried, what if I lose my benefits? I told him I'm not sick and I didn't understand his other questions." I reassure her that everything will be fine. I secretly feel bureaucracy had gone mad, the information is all on file and Kathy's GP is fully aware of her situation. I sincerely hope that Kathy's benefit is continued, Kathy is hoping to move and start a home for her and the baby, she needed the benefits.

There are no other staff to accompany me to visit Marcus, so I go alone, consistency is important I tell myself. When I arrive, the front door is ajar.

"Hello, Marcus, its Carla". No reply. I push the door open I can hear music from the living room. I step inside, calling Marcus as I go, three steps into the hallway. A gust of wind catches the door, it slams shut. That is the only exit out of the flat, I am suddenly aware of my vulnerability, Risk Assessments are there for a reason I tell myself. I turn back to the door. Marcus's voice behind me causes me to jump,

"Hi Carla, I made you this". I look around he his offering me a CD. I mumble something about just opening the front door for the smoke, he knows I don't like cigarette smoke. We stand together in the doorway.

"I made this for you, I thought you could use it in your car. It's rock music. Not heavy rock, some Rolling Stones and Pink Floyd." Marcus looks so pleased with himself as he hands me the CD. I say thank you, how impressed I am with the way he's done it, all different tunes. The case has "For Cala, roc music" written in a childlike scrawl.

"You are so thoughtful Marcus, Thank you." I can see Marcus is a little embarrassed by my comments, so I change the subject. For the rest of the hour we discuss his visit to Grandma, Sports, the news and the possibility of a shopping trip to buy new trainers.

Although the visit has been successful, I made a mental note to myself, I have been foolish; it could have ended very badly, '*Do not place yourself at risk again*'.

WHO CARES?

The Six- Monthly Review

I cannot believe six months have passed since I first met Marcus, many things have changed. I gather my notes together. Today I have my Supervision with Bill, in preparation for Marcus's six-monthly review, scheduled later in the week. Bill has anticipated my arrival and produced two coffees and a couple of Penguin chocolate biscuits.

"Oh, chocolate biscuits too, have we had an increase in the department's budget?" I act shy, tilting my head I wink at him.

"Eh, I bought these myself for the occasion, but don't you go telling anyone or they will all want this treatment". Bill winks as he opens my File. I've been on the team for five years now and feel very comfortable in my role. We always start with a general chat about me, my family and Mr. Tom before we go into the case studies.

"So, tell me what's been happening with Marcus, so that I at least look as though I know what I'm talking about at his review on Friday." Bill starts to munch his biscuit.

"Well over the last few weeks we have moved forward in leaps and bounds with Marcus". I am without doubt proud of our progress, I explain how we have taken Marcus for a drive, out to the local Country park, how he had enjoyed walking, chatting and looking at nature. There have been three more visits to see his Grandma Elsie, she had knitted Marcus a sweater. They are now able to talk a little about the past, mostly the positive stuff, school, friends and his Granddad. There has been a shopping expedition to buy Marcus new clothes, I laugh as I described Marcus in the shoe store, trying on every pair of shoes in the store, including a tasteless pair of cheap bright yellow trainers. We also got him new Jogging pants, rather difficult getting him to try them on, so we got them on sale or return. To date we have not managed to get him to wear the new pants, new trainers or new boots. He has put them away for a special occasion and we've not been able to change his mind. We took him for a Mc Donald's burger, which he says is the best thing he's ever eaten!! We have planned a possible trip to a restaurant for his Birthday in October.

All the Care staff have too many cases, so we have to decide who and when people can be moved on to other service providers. If the cases are complex, we continue to monitor with regular reviews. Seven weeks ago, I handed the weekly Care Support to "Key Mates," a local community agency, offering local support to local people. Annie has become his Key worker, she supports Marcus on a one to one basis, Annie shadowed me for three weeks; for four weeks she has been on her own. We agreed weekly updates to be forwarded to me for the time being, its early days yet. Annie's reports had been very positive, things appeared to be going well. Bill asked a few questions about Marcus and finance. The local Authority now managed the finances, to Marcus nothing has changed. He still has his bills paid and is given a weekly allowance for food. Annie has managed to get him to visit a local mini market to shop which is much better for his budget.

"Well, I think you have done a great job Carla, sounds like this young man will soon be completely independent, Well done!" Bill closed the file with an air of satisfaction.

"Thank you but it has been a team effort, we all like Marcus." I have probably become more personally involved with the case but nevertheless it was teamwork.

"Now tell me, how is Paul?" he gazes at me with a mocking smile, I could feel my face going red. How did he know? Office gossip is the worst, I suppose everyone had been making something of it. Paul and I have got into the routine of taking coffee together each week, to 'discuss the case'. Only recently had we moved on to having lunch together, once just once!

"Nothing to say, he's been very helpful with Marcus." I stand up and pick up my papers.

"OK Carla, I will see you Friday at ten. I'm looking forward to meeting this Paul". Bill give another cheeky wink as I leave the office.

Mr. Tom has seen my car pull into the street from the bedroom window; he comes bounding downstairs to the front door. "Hello there, my handsome boy, have you had a busy day". I lean down and stroke him, can't remember when I started to have conversations with my cat, it just seems natural now. There's a documentary tonight I'm looking forward to, I put some oven chips in (frozen of course) then decide to have my all-time favourite, egg and chips, "maybe a few beans", I tell Mr. Tom. I decide a cup of tea is best. After tea I shower and get ready for bed, relaxing on the sofa. Then I hear my works phone, I meant to switch it off. Well now I have to check it, it's a message from Marcus. It reads 'Carla. No one to come this week, going away. Marcus.' That didn't make much sense, I tried to call him back, the phone was switched off. I couldn't do anything now; I would have to wait till morning.

First thing next morning I tried the number again, Marcus answers,

"Hi Marcus, it's Carla, you remember we have a review tomorrow?" I'm sure I can hear other voices, it's probably the TV set.

"No man! No don't want no support this week, none right......no one I'm going away for the rest of the week, stop ringing me." The line went dead.

I look at Alan and explain what has happened, he too has received the same text. I say, "I want to go around there, are you free this morning?" Alan shakes his head, sorry but there is a major issue with Kathy G, he had to go and sort today. Although my curiosity is sparked regarding Kathy G, I need to deal with Marcus first. I call Paul; he had a text too. We agree to meet at the flat, first I need to get hold of Annie to see if she knows what was going on.

I dial the number for Annie's mobile, a male voice answered.

"Oh sorry, wrong number I'm trying to reach Annie, Key Mates". I am surprised at the male voice.

"Right number, wrong person, who is calling please?" he asks. I tell him my name and department.

"Oh, Annie no longer works for us." He replies.

" What do you mean?" I challenge, "Who are you?" He tells me he is Colin and has taken over Annie's caseload since last week.

He visited Marcus last week, but Marcus had his brother staying and said he didn't need support." Did you see Marcus?" Colin replied no, he spoke to his brother who he described as about twenty-five, bit untidy, usual black hooded, jeans and cap. Colin apologises, he hadn't really taken much notice. My alarm bells start ringing, Marcus did have a brother, but he would be around forty now. I grab my car keys and head for the flat.

Paul and I meet outside, he agrees that the person couldn't be the brother of Marcus, we decide to go and see Marcus. The flat door is partly open, we stop and listen, one voice is raised,

"I fucking told you idiot; I want the money today. You better make sure that bitch and those other morons from the council don't come near here again. We have things to do man, you are going to get your money back, you is going to be a fucking rich man if you do as you are told." The man speaking has a foreign accent, we can't see anything.

"Yeah man, yeah its sorted". Marcus sounds scared. I call out,

"Marcus, Marcus its Carla are you there?" as I speak, I can hear shuffling noises.

"What do you want, I told you no support, go away, leave me alone!" Marcus sounds very agitated and frightened. I decide to bluff,

"Marcus, I'm sorry I thought something was wrong, I was worried about you so I called the Police, they will be here any minute, I need to see you are OK."

There is a loud crash from the living room, the sound of glass breaking. Paul and I are now in the doorway, raised voices, swearing, threats. Then two males charge towards us, they both are wearing hoodies and have scarves covering their lower faces. The first slams into me ramming me against the wall, knocking the air from my lungs. I don't scream, I don't do anything I'm stunned. The second rushes into Paul, he hits him with something, but I can't see what, Paul folds over grasping his stomach. The men run into the street, as they reach the pavement the taller one shouts,

"You haven't heard the end of this man; you are going to fucking die man!". Both men run off down the street. Paul stands upright,

"You OK?" I nod, relieved there is no blood, whatever Paul was hit with, wasn't a knife. Paul calls the police. I go to find Marcus in the living room, the room had been ransacked, the sofa pulled apart and the TV smashed onto the table. I can't see Marcus in the semi darkness, then I see him wedged in the corner of the room, huddled down into the corner, his head between his knees. I panic,

"Marcus, Marcus are you OK?" He doesn't answer, as I get nearer, I can hear him breathing. I can't tell if he's hurt. Paul comes in and together we manage to move Marcus to the sofa. He doesn't speak, just stares straight ahead. We assess that he isn't physically hurt, there are no signs of injury. He was quietly trembling. This was a nightmare for Marcus. I felt shaken and my shoulder ached where it had impacted with the corner of the wall. Paul also looked shaken and a closer look at his stomach showed developing bruises.

"God man, those are Bad Ass people Marcus, what are they doing here?" Paul looks at Marcus, who is definitely not going to speak to anyone, he has a glazed expression, staring through us. I hear myself saying to Marcus,

"I'm sorry, so sorry, I'm really sorry this has happened."

I feel as though I am responsible, the department, society has let him down. Paul lights a cigarette and places it into Marcus's mouth, it falls to the floor.

Five minutes later a Community Police Officer arrives, followed directly by two Policemen. A quick response as they were in the area on patrol. They ask us questions, we are unable to give much information, we relay what we have seen and heard. Marcus will not communicate; we explain his situation. The Police ask if anything is missing, we aren't sure, Marcus still had some cash his wallet on the table, about five pounds. Did he have anything of value anywhere else? I remember Marcus kept things that are important to him in the cupboard under the stairs. We look, one empty box of trainers, one empty box of leather boots and one empty sports carrier bag, with a receipt for jogging pants.

I Sigh, "Well it looks as though they got some new footwear and joggers, about one hundred- and fifty-pounds worth." I feel a surge of anger.

The large, overweight, Community Policeman, explains what he believes has happened,

"There is an issue with drug gangs in the area, their latest activities include preying on vulnerable people, people like Marcus who are isolated. We have termed this, 'Cuckooing', they identify the people and then move in with them, offering friendship whilst taking control, they then operate their drug deals from the premises."

The Officer presents Paul and I with a leaflet. It explains how through violence and abuse, criminals are getting vulnerable people and children to act as couriers for drugs and cash, taking over their victim's homes as a base for their dealings. Frequently the victims are too frightened to do anything. The leaflet gives confidential phone lines to report anything suspicious or if you are concerned about your own safety.

The Policemen make notes and we realise there is little they can do; we have no real descriptions and Marcus cannot speak or refuses to speak. Its agreed that the Community Police will include Marcus in their daily checks of the area, they don't feel the criminals will be back for a while, now their presence has been logged. Marcus is instructed to remain indoors, not to open the door unless the code word "Butterfly" is used, if he has any concerns, he is to ring the number on the leaflet and the Police will attend immediately. Of course, none of us are sure if Marcus is listening or if he understands. The Police leave.

Paul looks at me and shakes his head,

"This isn't good, I'm not convinced we've seen the back of these scum, I think Marcus is too much of an easy target. Marcus, are you listening? We need you to speak to us. Marcus, I think you should come back with me to Briarwood Court, you can have your old room back until we find somewhere else. You will be safe there."

Marcus didn't move, his eyes remained transfixed on the floor, his mouth barely opened,

"No, no I'm staying here". Finally Marcus whispered. It wasn't the best solution, but as a temporary measure it was the best we could do. Marcus would see this as a backward step, he had come so far since being in the institution.

I kneel down in front of Marcus, "Please Marcus, help us to keep you safe, just for a few nights?"

"NO! NO! No!" Marcus focuses his eyes on mine, there is no way he is going to move willingly.

Paul and I step outside, to talk about the next step and to allow Paul to have a cigarette. We agree that we will have to leave Marcus tonight. The police will do drive by checks early evening and during the night. Tomorrow we will have an emergency meeting at my office to discuss the next step. Neither of us are completely comfortable with the plan, we agree to text Marcus at regular intervals, more for reassurance, not having expectations of a reply. We try to speak to Marcus again, he is now sitting on the sofa, Paul and I tidy round, Paul puts the TV outside, its beyond repair. I look in the kitchen there is no food in the flat. I go to the store bringing back a sandwich, a microwave meal, a packet of biscuits, crisps and four cans of lager. Paul adds a spare packet of cigarettes. It's four thirty already, no point in returning to the Office, I ring in and speak to Bill, Bill is more concerned that Paul and I are safe. I ask him if he can attend the meeting tomorrow at eight thirty, he agrees. Bills day doesn't usually start until nine, after he's had coffee and a look at the newspaper.

That night sleep evades me, I didn't eat my supper, the glass of wine didn't relax me. Marcus is alone, Marcus is scared. I send him a text message, 'Hi Marcus, hope you are OK. Try to get some sleep. I will see you tomorrow. Message if you need anything Carla. Time ten pm. I have to do more, I will speak with my friend in the housing department, there must be other properties available. I roll over, my arm aches, a reminder of the violence.

Next morning, I awaken feeling as though I have just got to sleep. The alarm starts and Abba sing about Money, Money, Money. I switch it off no 'snooze' today. I don't turn over; I get up and climb into the shower. Maybe I should get the psychiatrist involved it, could help Marcus get a new home, he could now have a proper diagnosis, face to face. A place which was warden controlled would be good, with panic alarms fitted. I grab a quick coffee and head off to the office.

By the time I arrive my mind is full of plans and ideas to keep

Marcus safe. Alan and Mike are huddled together discussing a case, I grab another coffee and make some comment about Starksy and Hutch, Alan laughs and says "Who, that's? way before our time." Eight thirty comes and goes, no sign of Paul, he's never usually late. I try his mobile, no reply.

"He's probably stuck in traffic, you know what its like at this time", Alan offers, he can see I am eager to get started. I open up my computer, might as well start on my notes. At eight- fifty-five Bill's office door opens, "Carla, can you come in a minute please".

Alan jokes, "Oh, whose been a naughty girl then?"

As soon as I see bill's face, I know this is serious.

"Sit down Carla, I'm afraid I have some bad news". My heart starts to race, my adrenalin rushes, fear.

"Last night Paul got...." My mind's on overdrive, Paul, he has had an accident, that's why he's late.

"he got a text message from Marcus, something about Marcus leaving for London in the morning, to cancel all support. Paul was suspicious about the text so decide to call around to the flat." Bill was shaking his head in disbelief.

"Paul apparently tried to phone Marcus; his phone was off, so he rang the number on the leaflet, out of office reply. When Paul arrived at the flat the front door was wide open, so Paul called the police. Paul found......so sorry Carla, Paul found Marcus. He is dead. It looks as though he overdosed on heroin. There was no evidence in the flat of anyone else being present. Paul's been with the police all night." I felt Bill's arm around me, it wasn't real, Marcus never used drugs, why would he start now? My shoulders start to shake, it feels like my chest has been compressed, I can't see, my eyes are full of tears. I lose control, "Why, Why, Why?" I look to Bill for answers, Bill passes a box of tissues.

"Who knows why? The police don't understand where he got the heroin from, there were four open packs on the table, over a hundred pounds worth. Police are still searching the place; they think he may have more." Bill took out another tissue and passed it to me.

"But he has no history of using!! He was doing so well; his life was starting to turn around". I cry into the tissue.

"Yeah, it does seem a bit odd, however, if you look at his case file he has been around some serious dealers and users, most of his life. Something like this was bound to happen". Bill squeezes my hand again and I wonder how he can be so calm, so detached. This was a person, a young man in the prime of his life, a man that society had let down.

"You mustn't let this get to you Carla, this won't be the first client you lose, don't beat yourself up. You will need to be strong. You are not God; you cannot control other people's lives. You did your best, don't waste your tears." Bill's voice sounds matter of fact, no emotion.

"If you are telling me not to cry, I am sorry, Bill but I will cry , I will cry." I sniffed as I look directly at him,

"The day I stop crying is the day I stop caring."

Marcus was cremated eight weeks later. There had been an inquest, the verdict was suicide, brought about by a massive overdose of Heroin. There were no flowers, no will, no speeches just a short word of prayer. Marcus's Grandma attended the service, along with Bill, Alan, Paul and me. It was so sad, isolated and alone in life, now in death. There were so many things Marcus would never see or feel, I wipe my eyes once again as I stare across the cemetery. I feel an arm around my shoulder, it's Paul.

He smiles, "Come on, I think we should have a drink to remember Marcus". We all walk together to the local pub and have a sandwich and a glass of lager. Then it was back to work and another case. Marcus will always stay with me, in my thoughts.

That evening Mr. Tom is especially cuddly, he snuggles into my lap as I drink another gin and tonic. Loneliness is not being alone, it is the feeling that no-one cares, I feel tears start to prick my eyes. My phone rings, it is Paul,

"Hi, just wondering how you are after today? I'm here with an unopened bottle of wine and a Chinese takeaway for two, I could be with you in ten minutes, that's if it's alright with you?"

"That's be great, I will get the glasses ready." So, I smile to myself and stroke Mr Tom, "someone does care."

ISABELLA

Happiness, happiness, the greatest gift that I possess. I thank the Lord that I've been blessed with more than my share of happiness. A wise old man told me one time; happiness is a frame of mind. When you go to measure my success don't count my money, count my happiness.

Bill Anderson

At the regular Tuesday Allocations meeting we learn of new and repeat referrals, clients requiring our services. Work is distributed between the team. Five new cases this week, two males and three females. The males include one man for alcohol abuse, a repeat client who has been living out of the area, history of bi-polar and depression. There is one young woman with a learning disability now eighteen; moved from a foster placement into her own accommodation, to gain independence. A woman in her forties has been referred by her GP, following reports that she wasn't coping at home and neighbour issues, the police are involved. The client is reported to be violent and has a large aggressive dog. The final client is a referral from a family member, a disabled woman in her fifties, possible alcohol abuse and issues with finance, both of which have implications for her safety.

The meeting is informal and relaxed, we all have full caseloads, so no one is fighting to take on more. It isn't just the number of clients; it's the complexity of their needs. Bill, as always, munches his way through his breakfast, whilst the discussions take place. Each client's background is discussed, we are given a summary of medical history, mental health, domestic situation, current issues, financial status, risk assessments required, and what outcomes are planned with the client.

I am allocated Isabella, or Izzy, a name used by her family.

Izzy had been moved from her foster carer because she had reached eighteen. She had been given a choice of continuing to live with a family, as an adult placement. This would probably have been least disruptive to Izzy, she would have twenty-four seven care in a family setting, though as an 'Adult' her boundaries would have been more flexible, she would be more involved in decisions about her life. The second option was to move into a shared house, with females from similar backgrounds with similar needs. They would be supported daily by a team of staff. Although, a good option for some, many struggled with different personalities and the 'high need' factors associated with disabilities. The last option was the one Izzy had opted for, to live on her own with support staff visiting daily. Izzy had moved into a flat and was currently being supported with living skills, including shopping, budgeting, cleaning and generally keeping herself safe. I would take over the support which had been covered on a temporary basis by the Learning disability team. Daily support, would include regular reviews and progress monitoring, a straightforward, no issues case. Well, that was the theory.

The First Visit

Izzy is wearing Disney Cartoon pyjamas and is sprawled across the floor, with her legs tucked under her, sorting out the contents of her handbag. I have read that she is tall and of Nigerian parentage, born in UK. The whereabouts of her father is unknown. Her mother and siblings still have contact; this was agreed as once a week, but it rarely happened more than once a month. Izzy is stunning, not beautiful but attractive, she had a presence, her eyes sparkle, her hair is braided close to her scalp with silver thread; her smile, well her smile is just infectious.

"I had frog's legs for tea last night," Izzy proudly announces, with a mischievous grin. I'm not sure how to respond.

"Not really, I'm joking." Izzy giggles and returns to her sorting.

The support worker Alice introduces us.

"Izzy, this is Carla your new Support Worker. She would like to have a chat with you to see how you are liking living here." Izzy stops, looks up and in a soft, fragile voice whispers.

"Aren't I going to see you again?"

Alice has been working with Izzy for over five years, since Izzy first came into care system. It is difficult for care services to meet all the emotional and security needs of clients without a degree of disruption. Staff come and go, departments change, and client needs vary. It's unusual to work with anyone for five years.

"I was hoping we could be friends Izzy, Alice, told me all about you." I said with a warm smile which I hoped showed my sincerity.

"Will you remember me? Phones for You, I will miss you Alice"

This is the first time I have seen Izzy do this; she catches me off guard. Izzy hears advertisements, learns different slogans, usually from the TV. Then the slogans are randomly interspersed in her conversation, in this case with hand actions, mimicking a mobile phone.

"Do you like Mc Donalds?" Izzy asks as she carefully uncurls her very long, slender legs. I can see she would stand at least six inches taller than me.

"Yes, Izzy I do, why are they your favourite?" I watch as Izzy grabs handfuls of pens, paper-clips, lipstick, nail varnish and sweet wrappers, stuffing them into a large fake Gucci handbag.

"No, I prefer frog's legs. Mc Donalds don't sell them, do they?" Izzy grins.

"Did you lose something Izzy?" I wonder why the contents have been emptied onto the carpet and then stuffed back into the bag.

"No, did you find something?" Izzy stares at me accusingly.

Alice smiles, "Izzy is trying to find a letter which came yesterday. We need to check if it's a bill that needs paying. Izzy doesn't read or write."

Izzy proudly presents Alice with a piece of paper, which invites residents to vote Labour in the next elections.

"No, it's not that Izzy. Did you not put it in the drawer like I suggested?"

Izzy stands and runs into the kitchen shouting the mantra 'Beanz meanz Heinz.' Beanz meanz Heinz……. Returning thirty seconds later with an envelope containing an electricity bill.

Alice opens the bill, "Now Izzy this is for the electricity and we need to pay them thirty- four pounds. We can go into town on Thursday, when you get your allowance and pay this. Is that OK?"

"Alice likes Mc Donalds. Don't think you like frogs' legs, do you? Yeah. I haven't got any money though" Izzy says absently.

Izzy appears to have lost interest in her handbag. Izzy stares into space, contemplating what will happen without Alice maybe? Izzy's concentration or focus is about two seconds. Bit like a Goldfish I think, maybe she is just nervous.

"We buy any Car. Com' .... I need to buy some more of the chocolate biscuits they are really good. Oh, and some more pizza, will you be coming shopping Karen?" I open my mouth to speak, then Izzy laughs a real loud belly laugh. "Only joking Carla, you can come shopping."

I agree that if I had time, I will join them both on the weekly shopping expedition, on Thursday, to observe Izzy in a normal daily activity.

We say goodbye and Izzy calls out

"See you Thursday, 'have a Break have a Kit Kat', thank you for coming".

I smile to myself, well Izzy is a refreshing change, she has a smile which literally stretched from ear to ear and a terrific sense of fun.

The office is extremely quiet when I returned, which enables me to get on and write my report, I find myself grinning as I recollect some of Izzy's comments. Midway through my last page the office door flies open and senior worker Lacey, virtually bounces in, throwing her three bags across the floor. Her clothes look wet and muddy. She had an almost startled look on her face.

"You OK Lacey?" I ask.

"Yes, I have just had a bit of an incident that's all?"

Alan, who is sitting in the corner looks up, "What sort of incident?"

Lacey pulls out the chair and unceremoniously sits down, causing the chair to screech and groan. "A car incident, I have just been run over".

We all stare at Lacey. It is now obvious that she is upset, her hands are shaking, her hair is hanging in damp straggles across her face which is splashed with mud.

"Didn't see the woman coming, I just stepped into the road. Next thing I knew the contents of my carrier bag were strewn everywhere; I was looking eye level down a drain and my bloody knee hurt". Lacey pushes the hair off her face. Alan volunteers to make a cup of weak tea,

"But are you OK? Shouldn't you see a doctor? Where is the driver now, did you get the details?" Lacey stares blankly as we each put forward our concerns.

"I'm OK, the driver was very upset, poor woman. She said I just stepped out in front of her. Bloody waste of ten fresh doughnuts, my favourites, jam and custard too. Completely squashed in a puddle."

We watch as Lacey pulls out a bar of chocolate from her bag and begins eating,

"Going to make me late for my next appointment, cause my trousers are soaked". Lacey splutters between mouthfuls.

We hold a mini conference in the kitchen and agreed it isn't safe for Lacey to continue working. However, after much protesting from Lacey we compromise, agreeing that she can go to her afternoon appointment but only if she has a chaperone, to ensure there are no after effects from her collision with a moving vehicle.

I draw the short straw.

Lacey leads me down to the car park, explaining that we were about to visit an elderly lady of eighty-six, Maria Strowski, who is living alone. She is disabled and has been struggling to manage. Her family live in Luton and aren't able to help. A couple of days ago she had been attacked by a group of youths, who had stolen her handbag, including her pension. Maria had been treated in hospital and was today home, we would be putting some support plans together.

Lacey stops at a small black mini, I think it's black, there is so much dirt it's difficult to tell. Inside, each seat is covered in papers, mostly food and sweet wrappers, empty coke cans and half eaten bits of food, which are beyond recognition. Lacey scooped up armfuls of the debris and tosses it onto the back seat.

"Sorry about this, I *haven't* had time to clean it this week".

If this much trash had been accumulated in one week, I dread to imagine what a month's collection would be like. "Maybe I could get a quote from the refuge department for a clear out?" I say jokingly, Lacey ignores my comment and starts the engine.

Lacey drives with one arm, the other is consuming another bar of chocolate.

"Sorry, didn't have chance for proper food today" Lacey speaks through a mouthful of caramel wafer.

We pulled up at Sidebottom Street, a long row of identical terrace houses, with small front gardens. Some of the houses are homes to families, the tell-tale signs of toys in the garden, and chalked hopscotch on the pavement. Other houses are dressed in immaculate white net curtains, hanging neatly. Rows of small flowers lining each side of the path.

"Best let me do the talking, I think she is probably still quite shaken. OK?" Lacey is ordering not asking. I nod my agreement; this is Lacey's case. Lacey reaches into the rear of the car and pulls out a file, after a quick glance Lacey says, "Right it's number sixteen, just four houses along, we can leave the car here". I dutifully follow Lacey to the house.

WHO CARES?

Lacey rings the doorbell. I look around, the gate is broken, it didn't look as if the garden has ever been weeded, some weeds stretch up to the windowsill. The window is clean; traditional nets with a frilled edge hang halfway down the glass.

Lacey rings the bell again, saying, "I think she has trouble walking, so best allow a bit of time." I nod.

The door opens; a large lady fills the doorway, dressed in a floral cotton skirt and a neat twin set of lavender blue. The lady stares at us. Her hair is tied back in a neat bun. She looks extremely well considering her age and recent trauma, although she looks a little nervous, managing a thin smile.

Lacey quickly introduces us both and explains that we have come from Social Services, Lacey presents her official card.

Lacey continues her formal introductory speech,

"We are to visiting you to find out if we can help you, we would like to talk with you and explain what help we can offer".

Maria Strowski looks first at Lacey then at me, slowly assessing us, then asks. "Is there going to be some sort of charge, costs involved for this help?"

Lacey is in her best kind social worker mode. "Not at all, we have access to teams of voluntary workers, who can help with the garden, repair your gate, get rubbish removed. We would like to chat about other needs we may be able to help with." Lacey explains.

Maria smiles as she stepped back into the hallway. "You'd better come in then". She said.

Two cups of tea and half a packet of custard creams later, Lacey had a full scheduled plan of action, which she confirms to Maria.

"So, Maria, we can arrange for a member of staff to visit every day, yes, including weekends. They will help you with any personal care needs, assist to get you breakfast. If you need help to go shopping, we can also do this. If you have further hospital appointments, we can arrange for transport. Now, you said that you needed a replacement bed as yours is broken. I can arrange for a bed to be supplied. The beds are not new but are clean and in excellent condition, we can arrange for one to be delivered. You said you find it hard to manage on your pension, we have access to the food bank at St Christopher's Church, a member of staff can collect a bag of groceries for you each week. How does this sound Maria?"

Maria is staring at Lacey, "Well, I think this is wonderful, I cannot believe you have just come along and offered all this help. I don't deserve it, its very kind of you both".

Lacey smiles a reassuring smile and continues "I will put everything in a letter so you know the times support will call, when the bed will be delivered and how you can contact me if there are any problems. For now, I will leave you my card". We both thank Maria for the tea, promising that everything will be put in place by the following Monday. Maria appears very happy.

Lacey climbs into the car, as she stretches over to open my door, I noticed a young woman walking towards Maria, who is still watching us from the doorstep. The woman calls out to Maria. "Hi Mum, I got those sausages you wanted I will bring them around in a minute". I climb into the car; Lacey starts the engine.

I look at Lacey. "I thought you said Mary has no family here?" Lacey nods and starts to move the car forward.

"Well I'm pretty sure that woman just called her mum". Lacey brakes, causing the papers on the back seat to topple on to the floor. Lacey rummages through the papers, grabs the relevant form, "That's right, family live in Luton." Lacey passes the papers over to me.

I stare in amazement, "Maria Strowski lives at number fourteen, not sixteen, so who the hell have we just been talking to?" I cannot help it, I start to laugh, Lacey's face is a picture, she is red, white and red again. Lacey accelerates forward, with a cry of, "Let's get out of here".

Maria Strowski did get a phone call from Lacey and a visit the following day....as for the other lady, she is probably still waiting for her Fairy Godmothers to return! I'm not sure if Lacey ever admitted her mistake to the lady at number sixteen.

The Second Visit

I agreed to meet Alice and Izzy in town, I had a gap of two hours before my next client. I prefer to call the people we see Clients; some staff refer to them as 'Service Users', I was never keen on this term, too obvious. I am greeted like a long-lost friend by Izzy, who runs towards me and gives me an enormous hug, squeezing my head against her chest, so my breathing ceases for a second. Izzy is wearing a pair of skin-tight leggings in zebra print, vibrant pink and black. Her sweater is of the same vibrant pink, fluffy and a slightly bigger size so it drapes off her shoulders, leaving her skin exposed. Alice is busy sorting out papers.

"Hi Carla. Sorry, Izzy has mixed up the bills again and I can't see which have been paid. I think I will have to go speak with the Electricity Supplier and arrange for the bills to be paid by direct debit. That way Izzy doesn't have to worry. Probably take me a few minutes to set it up".

Izzy is already looking restless. "Would you please take Izzy into the market and I will meet you there? Izzy needs to buy two frozen Pizzas from the Freezer stall, Izzy knows where." Alice looked flustered. I agree to the plan.

Izzy and I set off to the old market hall, it isn't large, it holds about thirty stalls selling everything from plumbing accessories to cream cakes, socks to bedding. All the goods are colourfully arranged on neat stalls, standing in rows up and down the hall. The market looks and smells exactly the same as it probably did a hundred years. The aroma of freshly baked bread, coffee and bacon greets you at the door. It is a welcoming place. As soon as we enter, Izzy shouts and waves to the first stall holder, a man in his sixties rearranging a stack of second-hand books. "Hello" Izzy shouts waving madly, the man turns calling "Hello" and he waves back. Izzy does this with all the stall holders; each one smiles calls 'Hello' and waves. As we walk around, I can feel myself smiling, Izzy doesn't know any of these people, but she brings a smile to all their faces. Finally, we reach the Pizza stall and Izzy selects two twelve-inch pizzas, she takes out a five-pound note, the stallholder looks at Izzy, "Sorry my dear, it's six pounds twenty". Izzy looks at her, stares at me and panic sweeps across her face. Izzy thrust her purse at me.

"A Mars a day helps you work rest and play, I don't understand. You tell her."

I take Izzy's purse and carefully count out the additional one pound twenty -pence. "It's OK Izzy, we just need to give the lady a little bit more money, see now we have six pounds twenty". I turn and pass the money over to the woman, who nods in a sympathetic, 'I understand dear way'.

Izzy moves on to the next stall which sells make-up, she is busily selecting a new colour lipstick, opting for one in the same vibrant pink as her sweater. It's clear Izzy had no interest in money, only things. The actual value of things are irrelevant to Izzy. Izzy doesn't understand money, her file said she had a learning development age of eight to nine years, most eight to nine year olds can do some basic arithmetic? This was an area we would need to work on, it made Izzy extremely vulnerable to unscrupulous people.

Alice returns and once the lipstick has been purchased,

she suggests we head for a coffee. Izzy states that she wants a Latte with two sugars. During the coffee Alice explains that Izzy wants to upgrade her mobile phone. It's interesting, Izzy can understand her phone but not basic sums. Izzy can download music and take photographs. In fact, Izzy knows more about her mobile than I know about mine. After coffee we walk to the phone shop, Izzy has spent several minutes testing out the new vibrant lipstick; with a few minor adjustments by Alice, using a wet wipe; Izzy now had larger than life bright pink lips.

Izzy marches confidently up to the counter and offers her smile; Alice explains to the two rather glamorous assistants that Izzy is looking to upgrade her phone. The first girl looks directly at Izzy and asks, "Are you looking for analogue or digital, how much memory do you need?" Izzy just stares with her mouth ajar, as she turns her eye contact to mine, she says, "It's the real thing, Coke a Cola. I don't know."

"I think Izzy would like the type of phone she already has but an upgrade to a newer model." I explain. The two girls glance at each other, the second one tossing her hair extension over her shoulder, looks at Izzy and asks,

"Do you use your camera?" Izzy nods and give them both a large smile with her pink lipstick. The second girl continues, she has a *why are you wasting my time* ' look on her face and her eyes fix on Izzy.

"So, do you need dual SIM? Roaming? How much RAM would you like?" pausing to take a breath, the first girl continues. "How much internal storage do you need, 8GB, 16GB or 32GB".

Both girls now stand with hands on hips watching Izzy. I want to slap them both for being incredibly bitchy. However, that would have been unprofessional. So, I say, "Izzy, I think we can do much better that this, don't waste your time here, come along. We can go to the more professional phone shop in the precinct". Alice nods agreement.

We march out of the shop, both linking Izzy. Once outside Izzy whispers, "Those girls aren't very nice, are they? I don't like them"

Both Alice and I agree the girls are not nice. They aren't doing their job correctly. I look back through the window to see both girls smirking and whispering to each other, Izzy's eyes follow mine. Both the girls and Izzy make eye contact, Izzy immediately gives them her biggest smile, waves and shouts at the top of her voice,

"Bye, 8 out of 10 cats prefer whiskers, Bye." Both Alice and I laugh out loud, how appropriate. "Come on Izzy, you are a star." We both link her and walk down the street.

I realise how difficult life is for Izzy, she is very pretty and very vulnerable, all six - feet of her. If she wore a plastic bin bag, she would still manage to look chic. She is incredibly friendly, too much so, Izzy hasn't learnt the 'rules' of society, to Izzy everyone is a friend, everyone deserves a hug, whether it's the waitress serving her coffee or the driver of the bus. However, Izzy does realise when people treat her differently, like a child in the playground, Izzy recognises nasty and spiteful people. It is this that Izzy cannot handle; Izzy wants everyone to be nice. Izzy it appears never holds a grudge.

I am already forming a fond liking for my new client. I want to ensure Izzy is safe and that she had the best opportunities to live a good life.

The Sixth Visit

Izzy is doing well, she is now managing her weekly budget better, eating more sensibly and keeping her flat reasonably tidy. I continue working with Izzy. This visit we were going to the Dentist, unfortunately, Izzy did not have good dental hygiene, as a result her teeth are suffering, so I have arranged a visit to the dentist. There are no dental records available, so this will be a first for Izzy.

Izzy is ready when I arrive, looking stunning in a shiny emerald green, short zipper jacket, skin-tight purple jeans and a large leopard skin handbag. The bag is large enough to carry clothes for a weekend away, Izzy carries a lipstick and small purse in it. Izzy's hair is loose and backcombed to a perfect round afro ball. A replica style my favourite singer Diana Ross wore in the early nineteen seventies. This of course was before Izzy was born.

Once the car is parked up, we both proceed into the Dentist waiting room. Izzy appears fine, calm and mature. We hand her details to the receptionist and take our seats in the crowded waiting room. Izzy leans towards me and whispers,

"I don't like it here; I want to go home."

I take hold of Izzy's hand and tried to comfort her, "It's alright Izzy there is nothing to be frightened of, we will see the Dentist together, it will only take a couple of minutes".

Izzy 's voice rises a little "I don't like it here; I want to leave". Several people turned to see where the protest comes from, including a little boy of about five years old on the seat in front.

"Izzy, it will be OK. Look this little boy is going to see the Dentist too, he's not scared is he".

Izzy's voice rises another octave. "I don't care I want to go; I want to leave. Because you're worth it". More people turned around, a few give sympathetic smiles. A Nurse in white uniform comes in and calls, "Adrian Smith." As she calls the young boy and his mother stand and move forward.

At this point Izzy stands up and screams, "I want to go; I don't like it here." Tears now began falling down her face, she is shaking.

75

"Izzy, please it's OK. Come on we are going". I carefully lead the sobbing Izzy out of the packed room into the car park. I cannot reason with her. There is no possibility of Izzy seeing the Dentist today, she is distraught. We climb back into the car.

Once in the car the radio comes on and Izzy stops crying, almost as quickly as she had started. It's the group Westlife on the radio, Izzy began to sing along. It appears the Dental crisis is over, for now.

When we arrive back at the flat, I try to talk to Izzy, to find out what had triggered such an extreme reaction. Izzy shrugs her shoulders and goes to the cupboard, producing a small cardboard box, Izzy empties the contents onto the floor.

"What are these." I ask lowering myself to a kneeling position beside her. The box is full of assorted bits, about five photographs, some odd bits of jewellery, large earrings in the shape of blue fish, a couple of wooden bracelets, two half eaten packs of sweets and a collection of keyrings.

"Treasure." Izzy smiles as she clips one of the earrings in place. Izzy then picks up a photo, "That's me when I was a baby, and this is me when I was five. Wasn't I cute?" Izzy certainly was cute with her large sparkling brown eyes and her rosebud lips.

"You were, you are still a pretty young woman now." I offer this compliment to boost Izzy's confidence.

However, she immediately replies, "Yes, and now I am beautiful, 'All because the Lady loves Milk-tray.'" Izzy starts to giggle, and I find myself laughing too, a genuine relaxed laugh at this innocent young woman, who has no inhibitions about herself. Her only fear it seems is the Dentist. I spend the next half hour trying to understand Izzy's fear. In the end I decided to refer Izzy to the Special needs Dental service, the staff are equipped to deal with Izzy's fears and Izzy wouldn't feel so intimidated by them. What really sold Izzy to the idea of a special Dentist was the Disney Stickers, that are given to everyone who goes for treatment.

"I think I would like it there; can we go now?" Izzy asks enthusiastically. I explain that I needed to make another appointment and I would let Izzy know.

The Tenth Visit.

Izzy had visited the special needs dental surgery without incident. She was extremely pleased when the Dentist had gave her a new toothbrush (Pink of course) and a small tube of toothpaste. For being exceptionally good, allowing the Dentist to check her teeth and then clean them, Izzy had been given four large Disney Princess Stickers. The latter of which were now stuck all over the leopard skin handbag.

Izzy attends social development classes in town twice a week. Izzy proudly announces she has made a new friend, who appears to be a very nice girl, two years older than Izzy, also with a learning disability. Both girls can travel independently on public transport. They had been spending a lot of time together and doing girl things, getting their nails varnished, going shopping and once a week going to the pub. My alarm bells ring at the prospect of Izzy going into a bar, however, I reasoned to myself that Izzy was nearly nineteen now, she is trying to 'fit in' with others the same age. I check on our records more on the new friend and feel reassured that Denise is a lovely girl, mild learning disability, she lived at home with her parents.

Izzy isn't up when I arrive at ten o'clock, she appears about five minutes after I have rung the bell twice. Dressed in pink flamingo print pyjamas with fluffy pink slippers, her hair is scraped off her face into a haphazard bun. Izzy is yawning as she opens the door. She smiles and steps back. "I didn't know you were coming." She groans.

I explain I have left a voice message on Izzy's new phone, to let her know I was coming a day earlier.

"Oh, I didn't listen to it." Izzy mutters as she sprawls out on the sofa and plays back my message, she starts to giggle, "It doesn't sound like you, it sounds like a robot" Izzy finds this very amusing.

I then let Izzy record a message to me, which I promptly play back....'Hello, hello it's me Izzy, Is that you Carla. I am sending you this message, 'Snap, Crackle and Pop', I hope you get it, love from Izzy'. Izzy laughs and replays the message, after the sixth replay I retrieve my phone and delete the message.

I am smiling at the pure joy Izzy is getting from such simple things. Izzy then offers to make me a coffee, white with no sugar. It arrives ten minutes later as tea with two sugars. Izzy apologises saying this is what Alice drinks, she had forgotten it was for me. I didn't request another cup. Izzy starts to tell me about her new friend Denise. Denise is great, she had nice hair, blonde. Denise made her laugh, she was always saying things that were funny, when I ask for an example Izzy can't remember. Then Izzy announces Denise had a boyfriend,

"Oh, ssh!! not supposed to tell anyone, please don't tell Denise's mum, no one is supposed to know." Izzy relaxes when I promised complete secrecy. I ask if Izzy had met Denise's boyfriend and what he's like. Izzy gives a detailed description of the young man, tall, nice brown skin, big brown eyes, great muscles from going to the gym. He did smoke but Denise didn't mind. He lives locally though Izzy wasn't sure where. No, he didn't have a job, but he was thinking of going to college. He had no mum or dad, which meant he was an orphan, Izzy found this bit of information sad. I ask Izzy where she and Denise went shopping, she told me about the trips out and proudly held her hands out to show me the recently painted nails. They were of course pink, with small white flowers at the tips, the centre of which held a diamond. Izzy assures me these are real diamonds, I say it is a shame that two are missing, then Izzy laughs and says she is only messing about, they aren't real diamonds. It seems every Friday Izzy and Denise go to the Regal Bar in town, when it is very late (Izzy's description) they go to the "Club", a disco behind the cinema.

I know where she means, it's very popular with the young people. However, as with most of the towns clubs and bars there is an element of drug and alcohol abuse. A recent experiment had been conducted by the local Police forensic team. They had visited the toilets in several of the pubs and clubs in town. They had taken swabs from the top of the toilet cisterns. This was the porcelain site dealers and users often use to cut the cocaine. They had found that over eighty percent of the swabs proved positive for cocaine, a frightening statistic in a small town.

Izzy attends a youth advisory centre to learn about risks in society, pregnancy, drugs and alcohol. Izzy has been going for weeks, she is taking the information on board and appears quite mature about everything. I ask Izzy how the sessions are going, "They are good, we get free coffee or lemonade and at lunchtime there are sandwiches."

Izzy doesn't remember much about what the tutors says, however, she is fully immersed in the sex education talk.

"The woman, she's so funny. She talks about condoms; do you know what they are?" I nod my superior knowledge. "Well, she puts them on to a piece of wood, she is soo funny…. gently now, we don't want them to tear. We don't want those little devils to escape and find the eggs, to make more babies". Izzy leans over laughing, "Eggs in our tummy…. she is so funny." Izzy rolls over on the floor kicking her legs in the air.

Then abruptly she sits up, looks at me, "I'm not going to get pregnant until I am married, then I will have two children a boy and a girl". I confirmed that this was a very sensible, grown- up approach.

Nevertheless, I intend to check out this 'boyfriend of Denise's' just to be sure. Unfortunately, Izzy only knew him as Ike, was that a nick name? His real name shortened. He was going to be difficult to track down.

Not that difficult as things turned out.

The Twelfth Visit.

Two weeks later I learn that Ike had moved in with Izzy. This is a worrying development, Izzy has never had a serious boyfriend and it raises concerns about her safety, the risk of pregnancy and abuse. I decide it will be better if Alan and I talk to Izzy and Ike together. When we arrive, they have both clearly just got out of bed and suddenly, the young innocent Izzy has disappeared and been replaced by a confident young woman. Izzy is fully in charge of the situation. She tells Ike to go and make some coffee then sits down on the sofa.

"See he's really nice, isn't he?" she beams at me.

"But Izzy, I thought you said he was Denise's boyfriend?"

Izzy thought about this for a split second and replied,

"He's mine now, she didn't want him, I'm going to marry him, and we are going to have a nice house and two children, babies. A boy and a girl. He wants to call them Nigerian names, but I like Charles and Cindy."

When Ike returns with the coffee it is easy to see why Izzy is totally hypnotised by this boy. He is very handsome; however, his English is very poor. He can't tell us very much, he doesn't understand anything beyond 'my name is, yes no, hello and goodbye. This language barrier doesn't seem to bother Izzy in the slightest. He does give me his name and confirms his address, he is living with his cousin, he arrived in the UK last year. I said I would try to find an interpreter. We needed find out what the motives of this rather pleasant, good looking boy were.

Two days later I received a call to say Ike had been arrested, by the Police and Immigration. Apparently, Denise's parents were extremely concerned about the young man and had reported him to the police. It seems he was illegally in the country and had been taken to a place of safety until he could be deported.

All of which saved me a job and took away the problem of Izzy and her lover.

Things continued to 'tick over', I spent more time with Izzy and took her out at least once a week. Strictly speaking this wasn't part of my role but I tended to use my own time for the visits. One week I took Izzy to the swimming pool, Izzy couldn't swim, and I thought lessons would be a good idea. Izzy seemed quite keen. Izzy had a hiccup at the pool entrance, refusing to go in, saying it was too noisy and there were too many people there. This was the public session and shortly after the pool became quiet, with only four learners. Izzy got changed quickly and stood quietly, shivering at the side of the pool. In walked the Mister super fit Lifeguard the instructor for today . Izzy is transformed. She smiles and walks up to him, says something to him, he turns bright red and smiles back. I'm in the observers area, there is a thick screen between us so I have no idea what's been said. Slowly Izzy join the others in the water, it isn't deep, the water level only reached Izzy's hips. I notice she is clinging tightly to the side of the pool, whilst attempting to look cool and sophisticated.

One hour later Izzy emerges from the changing room, hair still soaking wet and clothes sticking to her where she has failed to dry herself fully. She is beaming,

"I can come next week too, Nigel said I will soon be swimming like a fish. 'Only the Best for the Captain's Table'. I like Nigel." The slogan was said with a deep Cornish accent and I wondered how on Earth she remembered them all. I help Izzy dry her hair and we agree a swimming lesson for that the following week.

Back home my own routine is like clockwork, work, sleep, eat, sleep. Work, sleep, eat. Occasionally, I wonder what it's all for. Now and again. especially in the evening, the loneliness which I fight to hide, sneaks up on me. I wonder if it is easier for those women who get divorced, they can feel angry, vengeful, a sense of 'I'll show him'. Martin had just died on me, one minute we were happily moving on, planning, dreaming. Then the cancer hit, within weeks our lives were completely transformed. Suddenly it was a constant list of hospital appointments, Doctors visits and blood tests. After five months we learnt nothing could be done, the cancer had spread, the prognosis was the worst, maximum life expectancy a year. In fact, it was only another three months before he was gone. It had been hard, like starting again, being a single mum under forty was hard, I had to sell the business, I needed an income. I shake myself out of the 'woe is me' mood and make a coffee.

I still have two reports to write and I am concerned, Izzy appears to be demonstrating a sexual prowess, an adult attitude toward her own sexuality.

A few weeks later I have a worried call from the tutor at Advisory Centre, she is concerned that Izzy reports her monthly period is late, by about two weeks. We both agreed that a pregnancy test will be needed. This is my worst nightmare, how could Izzy manage, she couldn't look after herself, let alone a new baby.

Six weeks later, with the tutor present I try to explain to Izzy what our concerns are. Izzy listens quietly as I described the process...." So, you see Izzy when a boy and girl have sexual relationships, intercourse, then it is possible that they may have a baby, especially if they haven't used a condom."

Jenny, the tutor, who looks about two years older than Izzy continues, "You remember Izzy, the condoms I showed you at the Advice Centre?" Izzy remains seated crossed legged on the floor; strands of hair being twisted between her two fingers. Jenny looks at Izzy and gently asks "Did you have sex with Ike Izzy?" Izzy looks toward the window.

"We just need to know, you are not in trouble, we just need to be sure you used protection, a condom." I reaffirm.

Izzy shifts position curling both legs under her, "We didn't make babies, but if we had, they would be my babies". I then show Izzy a pregnancy test and explain to Izzy how it works, so if you are having a baby the thin line will turn blue.

Izzy stares in disbelief. "You want me to have a pee on that stick? That is so disgusting. I don't think so. Beans meanz Heinz, Beans meanz Heinz. That is soooo wrong!!"

After an hour of chatting, explaining and trying to convince Izzy this was what all girls did to test if they were pregnant. Izzy finally agrees to do the test. Two tests later (Izzy drops the first one into the toilet) the three of us stand in the bathroom watching, willing the line not to change.

It does.

"If it's blue does this mean I will get a baby boy?" Izzy asks, staring at the plastic tube, with a clear blue line. Once Jenny and I adjust to the result we realise, Izzy is actually very pleased and excited. Jenny and I realise the full implications of this, all the possible problems and obstacles this result now brings for Izzy.

Izzy says "I think I will call him Charles Kingston Monroe, yes. He will be my special boy".

Later that day I had to arrange a special meeting, everyone would need to be involved, firstly we would have the 'Professionals Meeting' to inform everyone what the situation is, and then, hopefully, agree a positive way forward for Izzy. All the Professionals know Izzy and work with her in various aspects of her life. Her GP, Social Worker, Special Needs Nurse and

Psychologist, will consider the effects on Izzy's health and mental well being. There is a very real possibility that termination or adoption will be recommended. Both these options will horrify Izzy. The support staff, advice worker, the tutor at college, which she attended three days a week, are all to be involved. The latter knew Izzy as a person, her attitude to life, to learning, her social interactions, all the elements that made Izzy a human being. Seventeen people would be at the first meeting. This number would be overwhelming for Izzy, so the first meeting will not include her. This meeting is crucial, the main decision being whether Izzy had the ability to go through childbirth and raise a child.

The meeting takes place three days later, time is an important factor, particularly as termination is to be included in the discussion. For over two and a half hours we talk about the difficulties, read reports from professional staff, discuss the moral and practical issues arising if Izzy gives birth. Could she physically and mentally cope with giving birth? The implications of this for ongoing care. It was going to be a difficult decision. The basic unrecorded conclusion was that it would be better if Izzy didn't have a baby. However, Izzy and her baby had rights. It was my opinion that Izzy would want to go ahead with the pregnancy and somehow raise the child herself.

We discussed Izzy's progress at college, her improved living skill; her understanding of the situation. The support mechanisms which were currently in place. Izzy had support at home and at college; twice a week she attended her advisory sessions, covering sex education (*Not too effective it would seem*) keeping safe, personal hygiene and looking for work. Izzy's recent commitment to swimming lessons, demonstrated that Izzy was able to adjust and adapt, to different demands being placed upon her. There was an update regarding the 'Father' of the child, who had recently been deported. He had entered the country illegally and was looking for a way to stay, hence he had wooed Denise and Izzy. It was the general opinion that tracing the Father would be virtually impossible. Izzy had not had contact since the week before he was arrested.

That afternoon a smaller meeting took place involving Izzy. I had invited Alice along as she knows Izzy better than anyone, Alice is bringing Izzy to the meeting. Alice and I sit either side of Izzy to provide support and guidance. There are still nine other people in the meeting. Izzy surprises us all, she appears self-assured and confident. Alice has obviously influenced Izzy's attire for the day. Izzy looks older, in a smart black pencil skirt, pink shirt and black hooded jacket. The outfit is completed by pink and black trainers and the large leopard print handbag (the Dentist Stickers still firmly in place). Alice had helped Izzy place her hair in a tidy bun, wrapped, in a pink ribbon.

My Manager Bill,welcomes everyone, especially Izzy (whom he had never met before) to the meeting. He then described why we are there, making time to welcome Izzy and thanking her for coming along. He explains to her that the meeting was about her future and everyone in the room wanted what is best for Izzy and the baby.

"So, finally, today we need to consider what the best options are for Izzy and the baby and to then decide the best way forward. Izzy can I ask you .Do you understand what has been said? Do you have any questions?"

Both Alice and I had explained the options to Izzy prior to the meeting. We are still surprised to hear Izzy speak loud and clearly.

"I want to have my baby. I want to love my baby and for my baby to love me. I want to live with my baby, take care of him. I'm going to name him Charles Kingston Monroe. He will be beautiful. So, that's what I need to do?"

I could have hugged her, without prompts from Alice or myself she had stated her case. The people in the room were also impressed with this sensible, young woman who knew her own mind.

The room started to buzz as different people began to speak, everyone was momentarily speaking at once.

Then without warning Izzy stood up and shouted,

"Just Do It, I want my baby, Finger Licking Good, I don't care what you say, I want to call him Charles Kingston Monroe, Melts in your mouth not in your hands. I want to go now Carla, I don't like it here, I don't like all these people. I'm scared."

Izzy's calm manner had changed and was rapidly becoming that of a screaming banshee. There were tears now. The others in the room were stunned into silence as Izzy charged through the room, sending her chair and a side table crashing to the ground. Alice and I followed quickly behind Izzy into the corridor.

It had been too much, she hasn't even had time to get used to the idea of having a baby, now she is being faced with Adult decisions for the first time in her life. We had expected too much of her. Izzy needed time and support. I knew then that I would have to fight to ensure she got this.

After several hours of discussion, reports, assessments and risk assessments it was agreed the Izzy's pregnancy would go ahead. Strict support packages needed to be put in place and monitored. Support would continue daily, to include visits to GP and ante natal. Izzy would attend Baby Classes, to learn what was involved in the birth and the care of the baby afterwards. Support staff would be present at the birth. Following the birth, a programme of twenty-four hour, seven days a week Support would be in place, to monitor the baby's first six months, with regular assessments. The meeting also discussed Izzy's current accommodation, which was considered unsuitable. The area was noted for drug abusers and prostitutes. Local Authority Housing would be approached, under their special needs and vulnerable people provisions; a new home would be sought for Izzy. The actioning of all the requirements fell on my desk.

WHO CARES?

Visit Thirty-three

Izzy has now developed a small neat bump, she is still smiling and appears to be handling the pregnancy well. During the first two months she had experienced some morning sickness, which she had taken in her stride. Izzy doesn't cope with illness; she just took to her bed until the nausea passed. This visit is exciting, I was here to take Izzy to see a possible new home, it's only a mile or so away but in a much better area, close to nurseries and schools. It's a small two bedroomed semi, I'm not sure who is more excited about the viewing, Izzy or me. We travel in my car, Izzy is singing 'I should be so Lucky' all the way there, a version I'm sure Kylie Minogue would have liked.

Upon arrival at the house Izzy is quiet, we walk to the front door, I open the door. Izzy freezes, she looks at me, then at the door, then screams,

"Is this really **my house!!!** My house **where I can live?**" Izzy doesn't wait for a reply but goes inside, running from room to room squealing with excitement.

"It's got a **kitchen, a fire, a garden.** Look Carla, look , look. Charles Kingston can have his own swing; he can play in the garden. I can cook him Pizza, look there is a **sink.**" It was difficult not to get swept into Izzy's euphoria, we laugh together.

"I think it will be a while yet before Charles Kingston can eat Pizza!" I giggle.

Izzy clambers up the small staircase,

"Because the Lady loves Milk Tray, there is the Nursery, I can see the road, Beanz Meanz Heinz, I am going to put my bed here, with pink curtains and pink covers."

There is no doubt about it, Izzy is a very happy young mum to be. Izzy talks for the next hour about her plans; it is going to be beautiful she assures me. Unfortunately, Izzy's understanding of Budgets hasn't improved. I will have to introduce some stringent limitations on her spending. Priority will be basics for living, followed by essentials for baby. For the time being though it is great just to watch Izzy being Izzy.

I will be very busy over the coming weeks, the support is now rostered and shared between three members of staff, ensuring Izzy and baby are fully cared for.

Visit Thirty-five

My alarm sounds at six thirty, I roll over. Today is a big day. Izzy is moving into her new house, I am supervising the move, initially, with staff helping out later , once the move is underway. Izzy has been instructed to pack as many of her personal things as possible. The move has been arranged at short notice and there have been limited opportunities to help Izzy pack. Alan is on Annual Leave so my partner in crime isn't around. I have arranged a Removal Company, a local advertisement said 'two men with a van, no job too small. Local removals forty pounds an hour'. I had explained that the move was from a one bed-roomed flat with limited furniture to a semi just a mile down the road. They assured me that the cost would be maximum of eighty pounds, two hours work. The Men with Van are scheduled to arrive at Izzy for eight thirty. I aim to be there just after seven, to finalise any last-minute packing. As I arrive at the flat, I feel a sense of relief that Izzy is finally moving from this place. The car park outside the flats is full of large black wheelie bins, I hadn't realised it was rubbish collection day, I hoped we have enough room to turn the removal van. I already know some of the other tenants, they too are clients. Three client's had mental health issues, one is noted for his aggressive outburst, thankfully, these are usually verbal. There is also a young female whom we know had a cocaine addiction and had been giving 'favours' for her supply. Yes, it was a good thing to move Izzy from here.

I have dressed down for today, furniture removals are something I have experience of, having moved to a different property twelve times over the last thirty years. I often joked that I must have Gypsy blood. Jeans and tee shirt are the order of the day. I have also brought along cleaning equipment, cloths, rubbish bags and brushes so the flat can be left clean. The new house will need cleaning too a member of staff is going to make a start there later. I knock on the door. I wait. I knock again. I send a text message to Izzy. I knock again. Fifteen minutes later Izzy opens the door, looking like a rag doll, which has been put in the washing machine by mistake. Last night's make-up smudged under her eyes; her hair standing on end, as though she had received an enormous electric shock. Izzy is wearing an over-sized baseball style top, with the remains of last night's tomato soup spilled down the front. Izzy rubs her eyes and smiles, "Hi, what time is it?".

Inside the flat I realise that very little preparation had been done. I instruct Izzy to get dressed, searching in her wardrobe for jeans and tee shirt. Izzy quickly changes, though she still looked half asleep.

"Izzy I am going to get you a coffee and toast, then I need you to help me. OK?" Izzy nod slowly.

In the kitchen I make breakfast and present it to Izzy. "When you have finished this Izzy, I need you to take everything out of the drawers in your bedroom, and put them in the black plastic bags. Do you understand?" Izzy nods with a mouthful of slightly chewed toast.

I return to the kitchen. There are six empty cardboard boxes there which I have asked staff to obtain, I had hoped they might have started to pack things in them...but alas no. I start to place cups, plates dishes and glasses into the boxes, using newspaper to try and pack them. I filled another box with pans and the kettle. This left the food cupboard and the space under the sink to be cleared. I pack the food stuff into carrier bags, fortunately there isn't much, I make a mental note to ask Staff to arrange a shopping trip. I kneel down and scan the cupboard under the sink, there is an awful smell. I reach in and find a bag of potatoes, so old they and their bag have rotted into a black, stinking mush. I feel the bile rise in my throat as I lifted the contents out. I quickly wrapped the rancid potatoes in newspaper and take them downstairs, open the nearest wheelie bin and drop them in. Phew, what a smell. I return to my work in the kitchen.

Can anything else go wrong I muse as I climb the stairs two at a time, where is the additional support worker, she's supposed to be here at eight.?

I look into the bedroom, Izzy is lying on her belly across the floor, rummaging in a pink handbag, the sort used for an evening at the opera, petite with small sequins stitched across the front. Izzy is completely absorbed and screams when I speak, "What are you doing? Have you packed anything?" I knew I was looking at a lost cause. Izzy had put one pair of socks into the bag, everything else was still in the drawers.

"Awe, Izzy I thought you were going to help me! The removal men will be here in a few minutes and we are nowhere near ready" I give her my sternest look. I make a quick call to the office, was Shirley on her way? Shirley had called in her little girl had to go to the hospital so she wouldn't be in. There was no one else available at the moment. Great.

Izzy grins. "I'm going to my new house today." She touches her tummy and continues, "Listen baby, we are going to move today, I am taking you to our new house where you can have your own bedroom and a swing. But only if you are a good boy and help me pack". Izzy looks at me for approval. It's like having an extremely cute child who is misbehaving , but so cute you cannot tell them off.

"Come on, hold this bag Izzy, stand up. Now keep still." I tip the contents of her 'sock' drawer into the black bag. "Now you put the things from the top drawer in the bag while I finish in the kitchen." I return to the remove the out of date food stuff.

I hear a male voice shout from downstairs, "Is this Miss Monroe's flat?" The men with a van are early, this is a good sign. I stop and go to the stairs where I come face to face for the first time with the Removal men. Who are from this point on in the proceedings be known as "Dodge -it "and "Bodge -it" Extraordinaire!!

"Are you Miss Monroe?" the small, overweight, untidy and definitely unwashed 'Mr Dodge-it' asks.

"No, I am Carla, the Care Worker who booked you." My confidence in the no hitch removal is fading fast.

"Oh, well I don't think we can help you ere, see you never said anything about it being a first floor flat, very difficult all those stairs. Won't take on a job like this to much work up and down stairs."

I stare at him in disbelief, further heavy footsteps on the stairs and in comes 'Mr Bodge-it'. This half of the duo is tall and very thin, with a long thin face and an equally long, thin nose. He has a cigarette hanging from his lips as he speaks. "Bloody stairs, I don't do bloody stairs. Going to cost you a lot more. I ave to think about my back, got a slipped disc you know, bleeding painful. Can't risk it"

I stare in disbelief at the two clowns I have hired, what was I thinking, I knew better than this, what was the old adage, 'Pay peanuts and you get monkeys?

The next few minutes are spent trying to convince 'Dodge- it' and 'Bodge- it' that the job is easier than they think, there are only a few items, we could maybe pay a bit extra, the payment is in cash. Finally, I try to appeal to their conscience, poor young, pregnant woman waiting to move into a new home, no other

91

help available, all ready to move. They both stand and listen to my pleadings.

"Thing is it's going to take us longer and we have another job at two, going to ave to charge for the extra time." 'Bodge- it' scratches his head and stares into space as though calculating.

"Well, you did originally say one hour, maximum two? How much longer will one flight of stairs take?" I can feel my voice rising in frustration. "Can't say, depends." They said in unison.

"OK, OK please just get on with it". I have to leave the room I am about ready to explode.

Then 'Dodge -it' looks into the kitchen.

"We don't do electricals, can't take the washer or the cooker. You need professionals to disconnect and reconnect at the other end." 'Dodge -it opens the kitchen window and throws out his cigarette. "Where am I going to get an electrician at this short notice? "I asked, my patience is threadbare.

"Maybe we can help. My brother in law is an electrician, maybe I can get him over today. I can ring him if you like?" Bodge -it at least had a plan, I am starting to feel like I am being conned, cornered with no options available. "Convenient having a brother in law who is and electrician". I mutter to myself.

"Have to be cash in hand though, is that OK?" I reluctantly nod. Izzy has a new cooker it needs to be fitted and she can't manage without her washer.

Five minutes later Dodge -it and Bodge-it are starting to remove cushions from the sofa. 'Dodge-it' is whistling as he returns upstairs two at a time. Suddenly, I hear shouting, raised voices and swearing. What Now?

Bodge -it comes up the stairs, he stands a full foot taller than Dodge- it. Dodge- it and I stare at him in disbelief,

WHO CARES?

"What the fuck happened to you?" Dodge-it laughs.

Bodge-it pushes past and confronts me,

"Are they all fucking nutters around here?" His face is bright red.

"What do you mean?" I ask stifling a desire to laugh. Bodge-it pulls at his tee shirt, which instead of showing a white skull between two roses, is now covered in thick black, very smelly potato slime.

"Some fucking nutter just came out of his house, opened his wheelie bin, then threw this bag of shit at me!! Frigging headcase. He's not right in the bloody head. This shit stinks"

I can't hold back my laughter any longer, a sort of half laugh, half cough burst out.

"Oh…. dear, sorry I have no idea who or why he did this." I am almost choking on my stifled fit of giggles.

Bodge-it glares at me.

"He was yelling something about me putting my rubbish in his bin, bloody idiot. I would have clocked him, but he was a big bugger."

I mutter my sympathies and usher him into the bathroom. "You can wash in here; I will try and find you a clean tee shirt." I turn to see Izzy staring from her bedroom, looking a little bemused and frightened by all the commotion.

"It's OK Izzy, don't worry, the man just had an accident with a bag of rotten potatoes". I can't help myself as I giggle again. I ask Izzy if she had an old tee shirt the man could borrow, because his was very stinky. Izzy holds her nose,

"I know I can smell him, who is Mr Stinky? "I advise Izzy it is probably best not to call him that as he is not very happy at the moment. Izzy rummages through a bag and passes me a vibrant orange tee shirt, not perfect but it would have to do. I hand the tee shirt over. A moment later Bodge-it reappears from the bathroom wearing said tee shirt, which is a surprisingly good fit. As he turns to walk into the lounge, I see written across the back in large gold lettering 'Dancing Queen!'. Very appropriate I think, going back in the kitchen where I can laugh out loud.

I help Izzy load the remaining bits and pieces into bags. How can one girl, have gathered so much stuff? I wonder. There is enough make-up to paint the fourth bridge. Beads plastic, glass, wood, stone and seeds, of every possible shape and colour, Izzy is wearing five strands around her neck. There are earrings, mostly odd ones, various styles, large hoops, small hoops, round, square, with bits that dangled, sparkled there were even some that actually light up and played a tune. Izzy decides to wear these. I can hear raised voices on the stairs,

"You stay here Izzy while I see what the men are doing, put your radio on if you want." I leave, closing her door behind me.

I listen.

Bodge-it. "You'll have to go back a bit it's too bloody wide."

Dodge-it. "I can't go back you fucking idiot, I've got my foot stuck against the bloody wall. Ouch! Careful you dick head that bloody hurt."

Bodge-it. "Lift it a bit higher on your side, right now gently push."

Bodge-it. "I said gently, you flaming idiot, aghh!!! my fingers trapped, quick pull it down, now. more, bit more OK."

Fifteen minutes later the sofa is sitting in the car park and I am administering First Aid to Bodge-it, in the form of a sticking plaster.

"Can I ask you both to please curb your language, I don't want to listen to foul language and I certainly don't want Izzy hearing it. I don't want her upset. OK" I am hoping to appeal to their better nature.

They both looked down and Bodge-it says, "Fair enough Mrs. Point taken." The rest of the loading went fairly quietly, only the odd argument as they shuffled up and downstairs. The Brother-in-law arrived at eleven, he takes exactly five minutes to disconnect the washer and cooker. He explains he has to go now to another job, he charges twenty pounds for his services and leaves Dodge-it and Bodge-it load the two items into the van. That is everything. There are still a couple of bags with 'breakables in', I decide to take them in my car with Izzy. A member of the support team has now gone straight to the house and is waiting to let the removal men in.

It takes almost another hour to get Izzy and her bits and pieces into the car, a final sweep round; we are ready to move. As I start the engine, I notice Izzy's neighbour peering out of the downstairs window, it is Simon, a lovable giant, whose bark is far worse than his bite. I give him a little wave and smile, mouthing, 'Good shot!'.

As I turn into Forest Bank, Izzy is excited, the van is parked directly outside. The brown leather sofa is sitting in the middle of the front lawn. Dodge-it an Bodge-it are in the van eating sandwiches, it is lunchtime I suppose. Izzy is overjoyed and leaps from the car, humming the tune from her favourite soap opera. Yes, Izzy will be happy here, the house is new, it has been occupied by two previous tenants, but the décor is all good, she can literally just move in, at least that is the plan.

Ruth, the Support Worker, comes hurrying across to the car. I like Ruth, she is one of the older support workers, has a grown-up family of her own. Nothing is ever too much trouble for her. Her grey hair is cut short and she too is wearing jeans and tee shirt, with an apron over the top, a duster in her hand. Ruth has obviously been cleaning in preparation for our arrival.

95

Ruth also knows Izzy very well and has been involved with the family since Izzy was ten.

"Thank God you are here." Ruth puts her hands on her hips and leans forward to catch her breath. "I was starting to panic, where on earth did the two clowns come from? Are they for real?" I climb out of the car and stare at the van, "Oh no! What have they done now?" I asked despondently. Ruth explains that the Clowns have tried to get the sofa in through the front door; they couldn't, so they decided to leave it on the front lawn. The front door is easy, however, there was a small hallway, with a further door into the lounge, it was tight but aren't these people supposed to be good at this sort of thing? I walk over to the van; I really don't have the energy to deal with these two numskulls.

"So, what's the problem guys. Are you finished unloading?" Dodge-it jumps down from the van, a piece of half chewed ham hangs on his chest and a smear of mustard lies across his top lip like some sort of painted moustache. Wiping his hands on his jeans, he clears his throat, raises himself a little higher by extending his shoulders and says,

"There is no way we can get that bleeding sofa through that fucking door. We have tried every way. The doorway is too narrow, the sofa is too big. The only way you are going to see that sofa in that house is by taking off the patio doors to the rear of the property. That's it!" He seemed proud of the fact that he couldn't get the sofa in.

"OK then. Why don't you take the patio doors off, if that's what's needed?" I try to take the strain out of my voice, I really want to shout and rave at this excuse of a removal man!

"Can't do that." he snorts, and I notice a piece of ham is also wedged between his front teeth.

"Why not?" I am going into melt down any minute.

"Because" he looks at me as though I am the simpleton and

continues slowly, "Because, you have to have a special tool, to take off those doors and WE don't have one, so it's impossible."

I feel the blood rushing to my face, I can't take much more of this, "So what the bloody hell am I supposed to do, you can't leave the sofa on the lawn!!" My temper is boiling over and I'm aware that some of the neighbours have come out to enjoy the show.

He stares at me, removes the bit of ham from his teeth, he looks back at Bodge-it and says,

"There's no need for foul language Mrs. I have a mate who has a tool, but of course he lives thirty minutes away, he would have to charge if he came out. Cash only of course. Oh, and we will need paying now because we have to move on, another job. This job has already taken four hours, that's one hundred and sixty quid. As a good will gesture we can reduce this and will only charge you one hundred and forty. How's that?"

I steam! Like a bull ready to charge.

"You, you, morons! you aren't getting a penny, I am going to report you, you are thieving bastards. Incompetent to boot. How dare you. You, you can also have your friend stick his tool were the sun don't shine. I'm not giving you, your relatives, your mates or your twin monkey there in van any money till the jobs done". I was spitting as I shouted but I didn't care.

Dodge-it climbs back in the van and shuts the door. Ruth had been listening to the shouting match.

"Carla, Carla they still have half of Izzy's belongings in the van, including the washer and cooker". Dodge-it starts the engine. My mind races, I could call the Police, I could ring the office for reinforcements, this wasn't how it was supposed to go. I need a quick solution.

I opt for being a human barricade, standing in front of

the van I look at the demon twins inside.

"OK, let's do a deal, get the rest of the stuff out and I will pay you". I scream. They both climbed out of the cab. Bodge-it who had been quiet so far turns to his mate and says quietly, "Come on, let's get on with it, let's get the cash and go". Dodge-it looks at me and says defiantly, "We want half the cash now and the other half when we finish". Reluctantly I agreed to the demands. Ten minutes later they have lifted everything onto the grass. Dodge-it then demands the balance payment. "No way!" I stand my ground, "you've already had half, but you haven't finished the job". Bodge-it walks threateningly towards me,

"Best give him the money before he gets mean". Dodge-it shouts over.

Ruth comes across from the house "Its OK Carla, I rang the Police, ten minutes ago they are on their way". I smile at the adult Grady Twins, "So I think we will let the Police deal with this." I say feeling unduly cocky. They turn away, whisper to each other and in a flash are back in the van and speeding off down the road.

"Thank God." said Ruth.

"Oh, I wanted the Police to catch them, now they might not bother chasing them." I am disappointed. Ruth smiles "Sorry Carla, I didn't call the Police. "

We look at each other and laugh, linking arms we walk back to the house. We make a cup of tea. Then Izzy, Ruth and I sit on the sofa, on the front lawn, surrounded by boxes, TV, cooker and washing machine. I need to decide what the next move is.

Izzy is still smiling, though the excitement of the morning has left her tired. Izzy asks,

"This is nice, do you think we can put the TV on now?" The TV is sitting on top of two cardboard boxes, on the far side of the lawn.

"Sorry Izzy, the TV is not connected. I think you and baby might enjoy a lie down after your tea. The bed is in your room so you can go in there it's nice and quiet.". I hope Izzy will follow my suggestion.

My next issue is how to get the items off the lawn and into the house. I ring the Office, Mike is in with another member of the team Adrian, they agreed to come over to help. Ruth rings her agency office, they said they will send a couple of staff who are free for an hour. I ring Paul from Housing; he promises he will come around by two thirty. At two forty-five we have an army of social care staff at the house, Izzy is upstairs asleep. The team set to work. At their first attempt, three of the men get the sofa through the front door and into the lounge, accompanied by a lot of cheering and clapping from everyone. By three thirty the house is fully furnished and has a working washing machine and cooker, apparently Paul knows of a trained electrician, who comes and helps out for free. Mike states he had plumbed in several washing machines; it wasn't a problem. Ruth takes Izzy to the supermarket for basic supplies. Two other support staff and I sweep and clean, so the house looks like a home. We connect the TV and hang some curtains; they are a little short but at least Izzy will have privacy later. When Izzy and Ruth return Izzy is very excited, she begins moving cushions and testing the chairs for best TV viewing. At six thirty I say goodbye to Izzy and Ruth, Ruth is staying the night with Izzy to ensure she is comfortable and feels safe, another support worker will arrive at eight in the morning. For now, my work is done.

When I arrive home, the Mr Tom is waiting for me on the doorstep, he shoots inside as I open the door. What a day!! I look in the fridge, a frozen lasagne for one, it will have to do. The wine is finished, so whilst the pasta is being electronically modified in the microwave, I make myself a pot of tea. I sit on the sofa sipping my drink, smiling to myself, as I go over the events of the day, it had been an unbelievable day. I hear the ping of the microwave and decide to eat straight from the carton. A quick shower and I crawl into bed with my book. All in all, today

CAROLE PARKER

was a good day

Visit Forty-two

Izzy was now into her sixth month, she is thriving on the pregnancy, but for the sizable bump on her tummy, Izzy doesn't look any different. Today Izzy is wearing a long tee shirt, black with a large gold rose on the front, pink stretch leggings, trainers and of course, Izzy had her compulsory large handbag. This bag had Mickey Mouse stencilled all over it and is large enough to carry a picnic for four. The front zip is broken but this doesn't seem to worry Izzy, she reaches inside and proudly shows me her matching Mickey Mouse purse. Izzy has been to have her hair braided, close to her scalp, the tiny lines of braids run in a criss-cross pattern around her head, at the end of each braid hangs a small pink bead. Izzy carries this style perfectly; her high cheek bones are more prominent, and her slender neck looks even longer than usual. As part of her review I will visit a "New Mothers" session at the local clinic with her. Izzy had been attending for the previous month and feedback from her support staff is very good.

When we enter the room in the community centre, I immediately feel my age, the average mum to be is just twenty years old. Izzy weaves her way through the rows of chairs and find us both seats near the front. Everyone appears to know Izzy and calls out a greeting .

I'm not sure why I feel the mums are too young, after all I had been a mum at seventeen. I was completely naïve about babies and childbirth, there were no mother and baby classes for me. During the pregnancy I was only seen once by my GP, who made it perfectly obvious, he didn't think I was old enough to have sex let alone a baby. My nine months were relatively okay, I had no real idea what was happening to my body or my baby's development in the womb. No Google, no Internet, no classes and alas no helpful parental guidance. I recall the only advice given by my mother, "You have made your bed, now you must lie in it". Not very useful to a seventeen-year-old. I did marry the father, but his parenting skills were non existence. I would carry the baby; I would give birth and somehow, I would learn how to raise the baby. As the baby grew inside me, I felt relaxed and happy, my figure was of no concern, though older friends warned me to carry out regular 'pelvic floor muscle exercises' and to rub cream on my stretched skin. I did not understand the value of this advice until it was too late. My waters broke six weeks early (I didn't take much notice of my dates; my calculations were probably wrong). I wasn't sure what would come next, I had been booked into a Maternity Hospital, run by Nuns. My newly acquired husband was at work, so his Aunt volunteered to take me to the hospital, we collected my bag and in thirty minutes we were outside the maternity unit. My first impression was this is like something from Jayne Eyre. It was a small Victorian building, dark, with high windows and a rather grand entrance door which led into a large hallway. The walls were painted 'insipid green'; although there were lights on, it felt dark. A Nun came forward and introduced herself, she was very polite to my escort, explaining that they would look after me from here. The Nun confirmed that visiting hours were seven in the evening until eight. Only close family were allowed to visit. Once my friendly Aunt had gone the Nun spoke to me. "This way, have you had any pains since the waters broke?" I'm not Catholic, I had never spoken to a Nun before in my life and I found her a little bit scary. "Well child, have you had any pain or not?" she demanded.

"Err, yes, yes I had tummy pains." I said this because I thought that I should have had pains, it was expected of me. I followed the Nun into a small side ward with six beds, three were already occupied with women, mostly I assumed older than me. At the first bed the Nun pulled a curtain (also in the insipid green) around the bed and said, "Get undressed and lie on the bed; the Doctor will be in to see you shortly". I lay on the bed, should I have taken my bra off? My nightie was very flimsy, it looked great when I bought it but now, black, see through nylon with red ribbons *seemed a little bit over the top*. I was suddenly very self-conscious of my body and pulled the sheet up around my neck.

I hear the talk has started and I'm jolted back to reality.

"Izzy, can you remember what we talked about in class last week?" asks the woman at the front of the class, who I soon learn is Alwyn, she smiles in our direction.

"Yes, pains when the baby is coming, breathing like this…." Izzy does an excellent example of long deep breaths followed by rapid breathing, blowing out. Her face contorts as though she is really in pain. The other ladies laugh, not a spiteful laughter, they were laughing with Izzy not at her.

Alwyn grins and checks her notes again, "Who can tell me what we do when the pain first starts?"

Izzy's hand shoots into the air. "We count, like one, two, three to see how long between pains".

"Well done Izzy. Though I think it might be easier if you use a watch or a clock to time how long has passes between contractions at this stage". Alwyn smiles and the others nod agreement. Alwyn then explains they are going to watch a video of a woman in the last stages of labour, followed by the actual birth. Izzy instinctively grabs my hand and looks nervously at the screen. I whisper, "Its OK, it's a film, like you watch on TV."

I don't know how I would have reacted if I had seen the film before my labour, I would probably have decided babies were a bad idea. However, there were no films then. I just lay waiting for two hours until the curtain was pulled back and a different Nun was there with a Doctor.

"Good afternoon Carla, I am Sister Bernadette, and this is Doctor Collins, we will be looking after you and the baby." She turned to the Doctor who was reading a clipboard. He waved his hand at the Nun and she stepped forward and pulled the sheets down, I swear she gave a Tut of disapproval as she revealed my black nightdress. Ten minutes later, having checked my blood pressure, my temperature, coaxed and prodded my tummy; the doctor asked the Nun. "When was her last pain?" The Nun frowned at me, I decided honesty was probably the best policy.

"It was about three hours ago." The Doctor shook his head and wrote something on the paperwork then turned and left. The Nun smiled and asked, "Will you be having visitors this evening?" I nodded.

"Then I suggest you ask them to bring you a more suitable nightdress and some slippers, as you do not appear to have any in your bag." She gave the instruction without looking at me. I was chastised. My newly acquired husband visited for fifteen minutes in the evening, he left promising a new nightdress and slippers would be brought the next morning. I didn't see Sister Bernadette until the following afternoon when she brought in a plastic bag containing a cotton nightdress, with little red roses all over it and a pair of what I described as Grandma slippers, full slippers with fur around the top, in a deep red colour. So much for being sexy. Sister then told me I was going to have a nice hot bath to encourage baby to hurry along. I wasn't sure how this worked but I quite liked the idea of relaxing in a bath of bubbles. There were no bubbles. The bathroom was cold and dark and yes painted insipid green. Sister Bernadette came in, the water was already in the bathtub. "Come along Carla, get into the bath, once you are in, I will leave you in peace for a little while." Under her watchful eye I slipped out of my nightie and tentatively put one toe into the bath, removing it straight away. "It's too hot." I stammered. Sister Bernadette said that was the idea it had to be hot. She added a little cold water, I tried again and pulled a face shaking my head. Sister let out another Tut and added more cold water, her expression told me that I had to get in this time. Sister stood with arms crossed as I slowly climbed into the bath, it was very warm, my feet turned pink, then my legs; after a few minutes I managed to get down into the water. It wasn't too bad once I was in, though I would never normally boil myself!! Twenty minutes later when my body appeared to be at a normal temperature, Sister Bernadette came in with a towel. I got dry and returned in my new rose nightie and slippers back to my bed. Where I promptly fell asleep. I woke up just as tea was being served. The bath didn't appear to have worked. I ate my very unappetising soup and bread. About nine o clock that evening I felt my first twinge. I quickly realised that first labour pains are unique, they cannot be mistaken as wind, they hurt too damn much. Two hours later I was dreading the next wave of the excruciating pain, I cried out as another gripped my lower tummy. Surely this wasn't right? Maybe the stupid bath had done something to the baby? Eventually, the Nun I met on arrival came in, she looked cross as she spoke,

"We cannot have all this noise on the ward, you are disturbing the other ladies. We are going to move you into the labour room" The pains were so bad I didn't care if she was moving me into the middle of a motorway, I just wanted the pain to stop.

Five minutes later I was in the labour room, which I soon recognised as a room of torture. Firstly, I was helped into a gown which stayed open at the back, then I was told to lie back on the bed. Sister wheeled a sort of crane across. Hanging from the bar which stretched overhead, were straps, I didn't take much notice as another pain ripped at my body. The Sister was now assisted by Sister Bernadette and together they each lifted one of my feet and placed it in the leather stirrup hanging from above, I was splayed like a chicken ready to be stuffed. Extremely undignified. The pains took away any possible embarrassment. The pains were coming more frequently, I felt exhausted, they continued through the night. At one-point Sister Bernadette came into the room. She walked over to the bed pressed a piece of wet sponge into my mouth and said,

"Just bite on this when the pain comes, we cannot have you screaming waking everyone up". I didn't have the energy to complain, I just wanted it all to be over. The pains continued for hours, I cried between the excruciating pains. I was sure my stomach was being torn open from the inside. Was this normal? Was it supposed to hurt so much? I cursed everyone, I was here alone, no one to hold my hand, no one cared enough. The tears, the sweat, the fear and the pain became a blur, I told myself it wasn't real, I was not here. The sponge fell to the floor as a pain severed through my abdomen, I swore, I screamed, I yelped like a wounded animal. I was terrified, the big, brave, cocky, strong Carla was alone and scared.

Then both the Nuns were around the bed, in the dim light it all felt very surreal, my movement was restricted by the stirrups. I wanted to push, Sister said to wait. She kept shouting, "Don't push till I tell you". I couldn't control it, my body said push, so I pushed. No one told me about the pain, not fully. I wanted to scream. There was no one to hear. The Nuns went in and out of the room like shadows in the night. It hurt, I was scared, why did no one come? Why was it taking so long? I was hot, my legs ached from being suspended up in the air, I wanted, needed to lie flat. After a labour of over twelve hours my six pounds five ounces, baby boy was born, the Sister handed him to me. I stared at the beautiful creation, my eyes filled will love but my head said never, never, ever again, will I go through this!!

I felt Izzy's hand tighten on mine, I look at her, she is leaning forward with her head down between her knees.

"Izzy are you okay? I ask. She peers up at me and splutters, "Can't watch this, I saw it on the TV, they smack the baby"

Of all the horrors of childbirth this is the last thing I thought would upset her. It seems Izzy can handle the pain she will endure, she can cope with the physical contractions, the pushing, the breathing. Izzy cannot cope with the idea that someone might hit her baby. I smile to myself, well that is the least of our worries. Izzy watches the remainder of the video and coos as the mother nurses her new baby, which sleeps like an angel.

After I had held my baby for two minutes he was whisked away. I was cleaned up and returned to the ward. I asked when I could see my baby, Sister informed me the baby would be brought to me at feeding time. Later the Nuns came in pushing tiny cribs on wheels, delivering the babies to their mothers for feeding. I took hold of my baby; Andrew would be his name I decided. He was so tiny, with beautiful blue eyes and dark hair. Then Sister arrived and said I needed to breast feed, I explained that I wanted to feed the baby by bottle.

"Nonsense young lady, the mother's milk is far better for the baby, it's got all the nutrients the baby needs. Its more natural, it helps baby bond with the mother. All good mothers feed their babies from the breast." This was clearly something that wasn't up for debate and discussion, I had to breast feed. I spent the next few minutes trying to get the baby to attach. Then all of a sudden there was a loud, painful scream from the other end of the ward.

"This isn't my baby, this isn't her. Where is my baby? Where is she?" The woman in the last bed, under the window, was standing and screeching. Then the entire ward came alive, everyone was in a panic, Nuns dashed up and down the wards, their long black robes made them look like they were on roller skates, they flashed past my bed. I continued to try the breast; it was hopeless. Then I looked at Andrew's feet, I remembered I had marvelled at how long his feet were, this baby had tiny feet. Oops, *wrong baby.*

It hadn't been my fault, though the Nuns acted as though I had deliberately selected the wrong baby. The baby was whisked away and a few moments later Andrew was returned, he was no wiser to the fact that he nearly had a new mother, or that his sex had been changed by one careless mistake. From that day I checked his feet every time he was brought to me, I studied him carefully so that I could recognise him at a glance, just in case the Nuns mixed up the babies again.

The class finished and Izzy stretches as though she had been in hibernation for a month. She gives me a coy smile and asked, "Can we go for a Cheeseburger on the way home, I'm Lovin it, please?" I agree.

Izzy continues through the next few months of her pregnancy without any issues, her health is good, she is calm and relaxed about the birth and her house is starting to look like a branch of Mothercare. Izzy had three support staff each day, covering the entire day. Once baby is born there will be support at night too. Izzy adapts to the new staff easily and although she did sometimes mention Alice, it is clear that Izzy had more important things on her mind. Two days before her due date, Izzy gives birth to a boy, eight pounds six ounces. She is surrounded by visitors during the day. Her support staff are with her to guide her. The baby is in a crib at the side of her bed and is constantly monitored by Izzy. I call in to visit on day two, Izzy is scheduled to go home on the third day. Baby is feeding well from the bottle (Izzy had opted to use bottle instead of breast). Izzy is positively glowing. I rang her to say I am coming to visit and ask if she needs anything, she thought for a moment then said, "A Cheeseburger would be good, oh and a diet coke please". So that is what I bring her.

Charles Kingston Monroe is indeed beautiful, enormous brown eyes, surrounded by long dark lashes. He has a cute button nose and perfectly formed limbs, but best of all, he had Izzy's dazzling smile. Izzy perches on the side of the bed and offers, "You can pick him up and cuddle him if you like." Izzy then takes a bite from her burger, as I lift the solid little bundle into my arms, he really is enough to send any woman into full maternal instinct mode. I stare at this little miracle. I am amazed at how easily Izzy had transformed from single carefree girl to mature mother, Izzy takes to her new role enthusiastically and with such energy. I feel a warm smug feeling to see her like this.

My transformation into motherhood had been far, far less smooth. The main battle was the breast feeding. My nipples were red raw, they throbbed with pain even when Andrew was attempting to suckle. He cried continuously, he never seemed satisfied "How do I know how much milk he's had?" I asked everyone, no one had the answer. I had to stay in the maternity home for one week. I hated it. It became a daily test of will power between myself and the Nuns. Visitors were few, my partner Mike came in each day, he held Andrew, chatted for a few minutes then made excuses to leave. He had a darts match to go to, a friend had a birthday nks celebration at the pub, he couldn't miss. His mother had got him food ready, so many excuses. His family came a couple of evenings. Mine didn't. It was two bus rides for my family, they did however, ring to ask if I was alright and when I would be home, the nuns dutifully informed me.

I had been so relieved to get out, my great escape. The first thing I did was throw the torturous breast pump in the dustbin and sterilised my new set of bottles. Once Andrew was drinking from the bottle both he and I relaxed. I could now enjoy the feeding session, bond with my son, without the constant nagging. Andrew stopped crying so much and slept through the night almost immediately. This bit was easy, the rest was proving hard work. Mike was out at work from seven in the morning until six in the evening. He insisted on two evenings out each week, to attend darts matches. I was alone. The house we rented had no hot water, no bathroom. The toilet was down the garden and shared with our elderly neighbours. A friend gave me a twin tub, so at least this made do the washing easier. There were no 'paper nappies' all the nappies were made of terry towelling. They had to be scrubbed, soaked and washed at a high temperature. This I was good at and I prided myself on the rows of white nappies, blowing on the line. There were big, big gaps in the relationship, I spent many hours at home alone. At times I felt as though someone had stolen my life, my identity, I didn't matter I was a mum. I loved Andrew but he had cost me my identity. My temper and frustration bubbled over; I was unhappy but didn't know where to turn.

Izzy touched my arm, Charles Kingston was fast asleep, I laid him in his cot. Izzy smiled into the cot and spoke softly, "Goodnight Charles Kingston, you are Mummy's big boy. I love you".

WHO CARES?

First Visit (Mother and Child)

I have not been to visit Izzy since her return from the hospital, I know there is a strong team of support staff, helping and guiding her along the journey into motherhood. The agency staff took over when Izzy went home, she was still on my caseload for reviews and monitoring. It is time for her three-monthly review shortly, so I feel a visit will be useful for my records. I decide to just pop-in, unannounced. On arrival all is quiet, a lady opens the door who I have not met before. I make my formal introduction and she explains she is Kate, she is on duty until one o clock, today is baby clinic at two o clock and Michelle will be taking Izzy. We walk into the kitchen where Izzy is sat at the table eating a bowl of cereal. Charles is lying in his pram; watching his mobile turn the various animals around, to the tune of Old McDonald had a Farm. As the chorus begins, Izzy stops eating and mimics the various animal sounds. Once Izzy sees me in the doorway she stops, jumps up and gives me a hug. Our training suggested that 'hugging' clients is unprofessional and could compromise a situation, I choose to ignore this in Izzy's case. Kate says she would offer me coffee, but Izzy had just finished the last of the milk. I suggest I will be happy to buy some milk if Kate feels nipping to the shop, which she does.

The Care manual is on the shelf I lift it down. This is the book where staff write down what they had done with Izzy and the baby during their support. Any concerns or issues are recorded, shared information, means smoother support. I immediately count over twenty names in the previous week. What is happening, it appears different staff are being sent each shift, this is not supposed to happen. The idea is to give Izzy regular staff so she will feel comfortable and able to talk about any problems. I wasn't happy. I looked around the kitchen, there on the wall is a large, handmade poster, with drawings, along with numbered stages describing how to make up baby's feeds. Firstly, Izzy can't read, secondly the poster is over the top of the cooker, an obvious fire hazard. I tear down the poster. Izzy looks at me.

"Awe, now I'll get into trouble, I am supposed to use that to make feeds, 'hands that do dishes', Trudy will be cross with me again". Izzy appears genuinely upset.

"Don't worry, I will speak to Trudy. It should not have been put there." I look around the worktop.

"Izzy, why do you have two kettles?" I tried to sound casual.

"Nancy said I must have one for my water and one for baby." Izzy stands up and put her dish in the sink, stopping to smile at Charles on the way.

I pick up one kettle and placed it in the lower cupboard. How ridiculous is that, I expect Izzy is feeling really confused with so much conflicting advice.

"Don't worry Izzy, just use one kettle I will speak with Trudy and Nancy."

Kate comes back into the kitchen, "Tea or coffee? I got some biscuits too". Izzy grins at the mention of biscuits,

"Latte, two sugars please. Think chocolate, think Galaxy. Chocolate biscuits yummy "

I ask Kate who Trudy is, she says Trudy is the Agency's team leader, she comes by now and then to check on things. I make a mental note to speak to her. There seems to be a lot of names in the book, so many staff involved. Kate nods, "I know, that's what I said. Too many people giving too much conflicting advice, I don't know what's happening, so I am sure Izzy doesn't".

"What sort of things are conflicting?" I was starting to see a problem. "Oh, things like one person says Charles should be fed before his bath, another says after. Someone told her he can have rusk after three month, someone else said they aren't recommended. The problem is that every support worker has their own ideas about the right way to raise a baby, they then share them with Izzy who doesn't know which way to turn. Fortunately, I don't have children, so I just follow the basics. Izzy seems to cope pretty well when she is left alone, with just a little gentle supervision here and there of course." I thank Izzy and K for the coffee and tell Izzy I will see her at the review,

I realise there needs to be some organisation to the support. When I return to the office, I telephone Trudy, she isn't happy when I ask her for a meeting. So, I decide to invite her Senior Manager along also. I speak to Bill, my Manager and explain my concerns, "I feel as though the current care package is hindering rather than helping Izzy, we need more stable support, one to one, to help her develop her skills."

One week later, I have drafted my requirements, specifying the number of staff to be involved, the care plan to follow, with specific aims and objects to achieve. Izzy must be allowed to grow, to learn and not be torn by conflicting advice. I had hoped the Agency would have approved the latter; it appears this wasn't how they operated. The meeting didn't go well. The meeting collapsed. I went back to basics, spoke to other agencies, listed the specification and eventually found a company not only willing to follow the needs led plan but offering positive ideas for developing Izzy's skills. The first agency was replaced.

CAROLE PARKER

Annual Review

One year on Izzy is proving to be a good mother, yes, she is frequently late for nursery, yes, she sometimes misses the recommended bedtime for Charles. Charles is passing all the developmental stages at the right time; he is a healthy little boy. No concerns.

It would be five years before I saw Izzy again, my personal and professional life had some major changes. One day as I am driving down the road to my new place of work I stop. There pushing a pram is Izzy, with a young man holding the hand of a little boy. I get out of the car and walk over. Izzy doesn't recognise me at first, then she throws her arms around me, introduces me to her boyfriend, soon to be husband, father to Charles and Cindy. Izzy has what she wanted; she is living her life with her family. We stand and chat for several minutes, Izzy is happy, Charles is happy, Cindy is happy and so is Robbie, the fiancé, I feel very warm inside. "Well done Izzy, you have a beautiful family." I say as I wave goodbye. Izzy is surrounded by happiness, what more could anyone wish for.

CHLOE

Give me a child until he is seven and I will show you the man.

Aristotle

First Meeting.

Chloe came into the Office like a whirlwind, happy, chatty, bold and confident. I had no idea what I was about to uncover and where it would lead us. She didn't have an appointment, but Chloe insisted she needed to talk to someone now, it couldn't wait. I took her into a side office and sat her down.

"Isn't Pete in today? I usually see Pete; he knows all about it." Chloe opens the conversation.

I explain, "Pete has moved to another office and his caseload has been given to other staff, so I will be your Support Worker from now on." Chloe stares at me

"OK, have you read my file?"

"Yes". I reply.

Chloe is seventeen years old, lived at home with her parents but had spent some time living with her Grandma and sometime with her Aunt. Chloe had a baby boy who was taken into care at six months old. Chloe had been sleeping rough, she was found sleeping in the street with the baby; the Police had involved Social Services. The baby was then taken into foster care. In a few weeks' time the baby is scheduled to be adopted. I didn't tell Chloe I'm aware of this. Instead I ask her if she would like a coffee.

Chloe says no to a coffee and asks for a Coke instead.

Once settled I ask, "So, Chloe what can I help you with today?"

Chloe stares at me disdainfully, "Because, you know I have a son, right?

"Yes, is that what you are here about". I can see she is uncomfortable.

"No, I'm here because Pete said he would help me find somewhere to stay, I can't get my baby back if I don't have anywhere to live, can I?"

"But Chloe, I thought you were back with your parents". I have read this on her report.

"Nah, she's back with him now and he hates me, he's a right bastard, he is worse when he's had a few. But she won't listen, my sister told her she's stupid"

I watch as Chloe's facial expressions changes showing the child inside trying to be adult.

"So where are you living now?" I ask.

"Well last night I slept at my mate's house, tonight my Aunty said I can stay at hers till Friday, her husband works away, gets back on Friday. He will go ape shit if he knows I've been staying there."

Chloe gulps at her coke, spilling some on her sleeve, she tugs her sleeve up, there I notice the signs of Self Harm. This form of self-harm is a cry for help more than anything else, scratches on top of the skin, easily viewed, Chloe makes no attempt to cover them.

"Well Chloe, you haven't given me much time, I suppose we need to try and find you something by Friday. It will probably be in a children's residential home if I can find one. It is best if a member of your family can take you in." Even as I speak, I can tell Chloe believes this is a lost cause.

"I don't want to be surrounded by a load of kids, can't you get me somewhere, a place of my own? There's no way my family will have me, my Mam is still angry because James was taken into care. My Gran says she's too old to cope with me," Chloe sounds desperate.

"Sorry Chloe, your age means we are a little bit restricted about what is available. Leave it with me and I will see what I can do."

"OK, I'll come back tomorrow afternoon."

Before I can protest, she stands up and heads to the door taking her Coke with her.

"Make it four o'clock, to give me time to sort things", I call after her, I am not certain if she heard me.

I remove my laptop from its case and make some quick notes on her file.

I will have to investigate what options are available, this won't be easy. Chloe seems like a good kid, why had things gone so wrong for her. This was going to be a complex case, she didn't seem to understand her son is being adopted and what that means, there is no way she will be able to keep him. Tough on her too, being rejected by her mother and Grandmother. I read the notes, a history of self-harming, but nothing life threatening, started at school. School had identified Chloe's vulnerability. She had a learning disability, only through perseverance by the school does she now have basic reading and writing skills; however, her concentration is poor. Chloe's intellectual age had been assessed at around age nine. To add to her problems Chloe is epileptic and although her last seizure was two years ago, she is still at risk. There was no record of Chloe smoking, consuming alcohol or taking drugs, but she's obviously been sexually active. The Father of her child is unknown and so far, Chloe had refused to name him.

Something about Chloe reminds me of myself, disruptive early years, little bonding......was this why I came into Care Work?

My chosen career path was probably subconsciously imprinted on me as a child growing up. The interest in Sociology and Psychology stemming from my fascination with people, young and old. Their cultural habits, their dramas and their needs. When I was growing up, I was never told we were poor, just that we had no money. Compared to many families on the Manchester city overflow estate we were doing fine. The estate had been built in the nineteen thirties to alleviate the slum conditions in central Manchester. For the first time many families enjoyed, piped hot water, indoor toilets; bathrooms complete with enamel baths. They also became managers of their own small gardens, to keep their pigeon lofts or grow their vegetables in. Yet despite the location, nestled amongst the green and heather strewn hills of the West Pennines, many were unhappy, longing for the communities of the inner-city terraces, where everyone knew their neighbour and being poor provided a common bond. My family had moved here when I was around three years old, prior to this, the only thing I remember about my first home was the long walk outside, over cobbles to the dark, smelly toilet. My mother carried a special key to get in, I didn't understand why it had to be locked, there was nothing to steal and everyone had their own outside toilet. Of course, memories of this first house had been overtaken by memories of my Grandparents house. Where I spent most of my early years whilst my parents worked.

Looking at Chloe's life it has been very chaotic. She has lived with her parents, her father left when she was just a baby and never contacted the family again. Chloe's mother had a couple of new live in partners, but these relationships didn't work out. Chloe lived with her Grandmother on a part time basis for about four years, then she went to stay with her Aunt and Uncle, her Mother's sister. The last five years have been the most chaotic, Chloe started to stay out a lot at various friends, no one knew where she was or who she was with, Chloe just said she stayed with mates.

We had taken up residency in our new home in 1959, it was a semi with three bedrooms, a small kitchen, an indoor toilet, a bathroom which was literally a room for a bath, there was no space for anything else, a wooden rack was suspended over the bath where in bad weather the weekly wash hung to dry. In the main living room was a black leaded Range, incorporating an open fire, warming cupboard and oven. The oven was never to my knowledge used for cooking but sometimes socks and underwear were placed in the warming cupboard, to 'air' or finish drying. On Sundays home made rice pudding was kept warm in the range, where a lovely crusty skin would form on top; my siblings and I would quarrel for pieces of 'skin'. As a young child growing up there, life was an adventure, so much to explore. The average family had between six and twelve children, the largest houses had three bedrooms and I often wondered where everyone slept, over-crowding never seemed to be a problem. I often wished I was part of a large family, they always seemed to have more fun, and more fights. My mother always said we lived on the better part of the estate, the posher bit. Plus, both parents had work, admittedly, not skilled work but nevertheless a regular income. This meant we usually had food available. Had clean and presentable clothes and the bonus of a small car for trips out.

Chloe has a large extended family, there are rifts in the family, some members don't speak. Chloe has grown up with several children in the house, three older brothers and an older sister. Chloe's mother was herself from a large family, the family's name is somewhat notorious on the estate. Well known for their petty thieving, drinking habits and general unsociable behaviour.

It's funny how time changes one's perspective. I don't remember any rainy days in my childhood. Most of my friends lived in the 'Not allowed to go there' areas of the estate, so they were the ones who were most interesting and most fun. One girl, belonging to a particularly notorious family invited me back for tea after school, although the house was out of bounds, I went anyway. Once inside I was amazed to see the family didn't have any furniture, the only seats were upturned wooden orange boxes, these doubled as a table. There was no TV, no curtains not even a carpet. There were five other older siblings, when their mother came home, she opened a large can of soup and placed it on the open fire for their supper. It was at that point I decided I might enjoy tea at home more, made my excuses and left.

One other family always stayed in my memories; I wasn't sure how many of them there were, but I do remember the younger one asking me one morning if I'd like to see their horse. I didn't believe her of course, how could they have a horse? She quickly ran into the house and a few moments later the living room window was thrown open and a full-size horse's head appeared. How or why they had a horse in their house I will never know, my Grandmother said the children had grown wild because their parents had gone and there was no one to control them.

Chloe must have stayed in some strange places, some of her 'friends' were known to Social Services, one had a history of drugs and alcohol abuse. All the 'friends lived in the poorest areas of town, noted for problems with the Police, drug dealers and general petty crime. Chloe was Street wise; you couldn't survive as she had if you weren't tough and resilient. It seems her Grandmother and her Aunt provided some stability, unfortunately this was short lived.

It was during the early period I felt loved by both my Grandparents and they created a stable background for me. Which was why at the age of eight I was devastated to learn we were moving away, I would be losing my friends, changing school but worst of all losing the daily contact with my Grandparents. My childhood experiences made it easier to identify the needs of children in care, the value of families, the sense of loss, frustration, inadequacy, needing to belong, to be loved.

Chloe needed support to get her life back on track, only time will tell if I can help her achieve this. This much I do know, Chloe is hurting, she is trying desperately to be grown-up, independent. She is lonely, giving birth so young wasn't easy and from the file notes, it didn't look as though she had much support during the pregnancy, or labour. The big mystery is, who is the father? Maybe Chloe didn't know? Maybe she knew but for some reason was afraid to say?

Second Visit

The office is busy this morning, Alan has been in a meeting for the last two hours. When he finally emerges, he looks tired.

"Fancy a coffee, next door?" I suggest. Alan nods and grabs his jacket from the back of his chair. There is a small coffee shop next door, we all frequent the place now and then to get a break from the office, the prices are more expensive but it's a nice relaxed setting with easy chairs and gentle music in the background. I grab two coffees.

"My treat", I wave away the five- pound note Alan is offering.

"So, what's going on, this is the third meeting this week?" I'm curious, I have rarely seen Alan looking so stressed.

"Its Kathy G, you remember you took her for her medical

119

assessment?" Alan says stirring his coffee. I smile and nod.

"Well we worked hard to get her a new home, set everything up for her and the baby, put regular support in. Then she meets Gary, who moves in after a few days. Not only is this against her tenancy agreement, this guy is really bad news, known to the police, a history of violence. Kathy stops co-operating with support staff, refuses to let them in. I go around and after a couple of attempts she lets me in. The place is a mess, she hasn't been looking after the house or herself. This Gary character is sitting there as though he owns the place. I tell Chloe I need to speak to her in private, he gets all aggressive. So, I end up leaving. I haven't seen the baby." Alan looks down in deep thought, I can see this has got to him. He continues,

"Went back the next day with the community police liaison officer, I didn't want to risk violence. When we got there Kathy looked terrible, she obviously hadn't slept. When I asked her where Gary was, she said he'd moved out.. I wasn't sure if I believed her. I asked where the baby was, she said he was asleep upstairs in his cot. At first, she was reluctant to let me see him. Then she insisted she came with me. Upstairs the room was in darkness, the curtains were drawn. I went to open the curtains; Kathy was really upset. I couldn't understand her, you know when she's stressed her speech is really affected. Anyway, I saw the baby. He had a red hand print across his face. Kathy says she smacked him because he wouldn't stop crying. The baby was breathing OK, but I knew I had to act quickly. I arranged for the baby to be taken immediately to a place of safety. It was really distressing, Kathy was so emotional, screaming at me, begging me not to take him. God, I tell you, it really got to me, I never expected Kathy to do this to her baby, she loves him, it was out of character. The evidence was there, and she freely admitted what she had done." Alan filled up as he spoke, reaching for his handkerchief.

"Oh Alan, I'm so sorry to hear this. I would not have expected this from Kathy. Where's the baby now? Did the creep Gary come back?" I was surprised and shocked by Alan's account.

"Baby is in foster care. Kathy is still at home, refusing support but we understand 'Gary' has moved back in. What a mess, we worked so hard to make it work too." Alan drained his coffee. "Best get back I've got two reports to complete before tomorrow, looks like Kathy might lose her tenancy." Alan got up, I touched his arm and gave him a supportive squeeze. Alan nodded a half smile and we went back to the office in silence.

I have almost given up on Chloe, it is four thirty when the receptionist rings and says Chloe is here. Unfortunately, I don't have any good news for her, I have checked out the accommodation for teenagers within a ten-mile radius, there is nothing available. Everywhere is struggling, there is a culture of 'Sofa Surfing'. Kids who are technically homeless, sleeping on other people's sofas, often the people they stay with have 'issues' of their own, it isn't the best solution. The best option was of course family and I have to try them first, I think the Grandmother might be open to persuasion.

Chloe is dressed in a bright pink tee shirt, white leggings and flip flops, it is only March so probably not the best attire. Her brown hair is scraped off her face and tied in a high ponytail. Chloe has a pretty face, but this style makes her look hard and her features more pointed.

'Hello, I had almost given up on you, are you " I say.

"Yeah, been babysitting my mates' kids while she got her nails done. I would have got mine done too but don't have any money. They stopped my benefits last week because I didn't go for the appointment, got my days mixed up. Now I have to wait and go for another interview next week." Chloe is chewing gum; a small bubble emerges from her lips.

"That's not good, don't you have a diary to put your

appointments in? How are you going to manage without any money?" I ask, concerned that Chloe's attitude to money is so blasé.

"Oh, it's alright, phoned them this morning they are going to arrange a Crisis loan for me tomorrow morning at ten, don't need a diary got my phone".

Chloe may not seem intelligent in the traditional sense, but she knows her way around the welfare system, the rules and benefits. She is most definitely a survivor.

I explain my findings to her, she pulls a sour face when I mention some of the residential places are ten miles away, clearly Chloe wants to stay in her own territory. I explain how they operate, the rules about behaviour, coming and going, noise, eating times. I hope this will make family seem a better option. I then ask about her Grandmother.

"Do you still see your Grandmother; she lives locally doesn't she?" I already know the answer.

"Yeah, I see her a lot, she is getting old now, can't do as much as she used to. I get her shopping every week". Chloe blew another bubble and starts to pick a small thread on the cushion.

This is positive, maybe Grandmother will be the best option.

"I'm going to make an appointment to see your Grandmother tomorrow if I can, do you think she would let you stay?" I watch Chloe's expression carefully; she doesn't seem phased by my suggestion.

Chloe looks sad. "No, she says she can't cope with me, cause I'm always doing stuff, going out, meeting mates. She said she can't cope with the worry. Plus, she hasn't got a bed". Chloe snapped off the piece of cotton.

"Well, would you mind if I had a chat with your Grandmother, to see if we can arrange something?"

Chloe shrugs her shoulders, "OK, whatever, won't do any good. Would you like to see a picture of James?" Chloe's face brightens.

Chloe removes her backpack and takes out a large blue folder with doodles covering the front, she passes the folder to me, then drags her chair next to mine to show me the contents.

The first page shows a new-born, all dressed in blue with fair hair. Underneath, a page from a notebook is attached with tape, the page is decorated with hand drawn flowers and teddy bears. In large childlike writing are the following words...

"On the day you came I knew you were the most important thing in my life. I love you soooo, soooo much, I love your tiny hands and feet, your cute nose and your big blue eyes. I will call you James, you are beautiful, I will always love you."

A lump forms in my throat and my eyes started to fill, I turn the page. (Be professional Carla I remind myself.) The entire folder covers the first few weeks of the baby's life, with short messages, "Hugs and Kisses"; "Beautiful Boy" written next to each photograph.

I quickly wipe away an escaping tear,

"I made this for James, do you think he will like it? When he gets older of course not now. Are you crying?" Chloe smiles mischievously.

"No just got something in my eye. I think this folder is lovely, I am sure James will know how much you love him." I smile back.

"Yeah, well soon as I get myself sorted." Chloe's armour is back in place she wouldn't let it slip, not now, maybe never. Her emotions are buried deep.

Chloe pushes the folder back into her bag,

"So, I will see you Thursday afternoon? After you have seen my Gran?"

"Well actually I am busy Thursday afternoon, but how would you like to come along to the meeting, hear what we talk about," I add this as an afterthought, maybe it will help if Chloe's there. "That's OK. I will see you Friday". Chloe stands up, pushing her folder into her rucksack , she heads for the door.

I Guess that is the end of the meeting. I return upstairs to finish my work, there are no computers available, so I sit in a corner with my laptop.

The following day I arrive in the office early, needing to make some phone calls. It is one thirty, I have just finished my sandwich and coffee when a call arrives. It's Megan one of the field support staff. She works with the elderly in the community and we share support of several clients.

"Hi Carla, sorry to be a nuisance but I think there is a problem with Ethel. I haven't seen her since my last visit over a week ago. Today there is no reply from her flat, you know what she is like, she could have just gone off to her sisters or she could have been hitting the wine again. The thing is the staff at the sheltered housing say they haven't seen her for two days. I am not sure what to do?" Megan sounds worried.

"Can't you get access with the key from the key safe?" I ask a little too impatiently.

"There is no key and the staff here said Ethel took their key last week, said she had locked herself out. They 'forgot' to get the key back from her. We do have an emergency key back at the office. I am really worried because her best friend Mavis, says she hasn't seen Ethel either. Ethel didn't turn up for their regular bingo last night either". Megan sighs, I suspect in part frustration, part annoyance.

"Thing is Carla, Ethel was on a real downer last week, she had a row with her son. You know how much she depends on him, he walked out in a temper threatening to never come back. It was apparently, a very heated shouting match, about money, so the staff say." Megan is closer to the family than I am, I respect her concern.

I agree to collect the key from our reception area and to go to meet Megan at the site. It is quite worrying, we all had a soft spot for Ethel, she is a character, a lovable scoundrel. With a colourful past which included her working for a high-class Escort Agency, also as a Croupier in Las Vegas. Rumours also suggested she had been seeing a member of the gang involved in The Great Train Robbery, during the 1960s. Ethel is now in her eighties, she has asthma, is almost completely deaf and she recently had a hip replacement. Ethel's been in sheltered housing for ten years, she had a history of alcohol abuse and smokes like a trooper, despite her asthma. Ethel usually looks after her appearance, she spends most of her money on clothes, cigarettes and wine, oh and Bingo. Her hair is silver shoulder length, with a streak across the front, sometimes the streak is pink sometimes blue depending upon her outfit. Flamboyant is the best way to describe Ethel, her outfits are always young, colourful and sexy.

When I arrive at the block of apartments Megan is waiting in the foyer. It is one of the better sheltered housing schemes, staffed twenty- four- seven, with community activities every week in the large communal hall. After our general pleasantries I follow Megan to the staff office.

"This is Jean the Manager and Fiona, sorry are you the Deputy Manager?" The younger woman looks at Megan and nods grudgingly.

"Right, well, we better get on with this, let's go up to her flat. I am sure this is a waste of time; Ethel is always disappearing. She goes into town visiting her son or her sister and doesn't come home. We can't keep a track of her all the time". Jean is obviously too busy doing her crossword to have to deal with this. The four of us walk up the stairs to the second floor, the lifts are for residents only. We then walk the length of the corridor to room 221.

It will be very embarrassing for Jean if anything has happened to Ethel. She is quite frail; she has never regained her strength, and since her hip operation her mobility had been limited. Ethel has two sticks to help her walk, she is so stubborn, always saying she doesn't need them. In the last six months, Ethel's taken three falls, the first she just sustained bruises and a black eye, the second she ended up in hospital with a broken wrist. More recently she has escaped with a cracked rib and an horrendous nosebleed.

A thought flashes through my mind. Do I remember the procedure in the event of a death, the Doctor, the Police, notify the Office, oh and of course her son? He is another person who would feel guilty, he rarely visits her, and he is an only child.

We arrive at the flat; Megan looks at me, bites her bottom lip nervously. I knock on the door. There is no reply.

"Come on this is a waste of time, just open the bloody door". Jean glares at me.

I open the door. The flat is in complete darkness. We all call out Ethel's name, I feel my way across the room to the window, slowly open the curtains. There is a strange stale smell. Everything in the flat looks normal, the photos, the vast collection of cheap porcelain figurines. An unopened pack of cigarettes is on the table. I move into the kitchen, closely followed by my three associates. Jean and Fiona are suddenly very quiet. The kitchen sink is full of dirty pots, Ethel would never leave the kitchen in a mess, it is completely out of character. There is a full cup of tea on the table and a half-eaten sandwich which had curled with age.

"Ethel, it's me Megan, Ethel are you here?" Megan looked terrified. I'm none too happy; I have only dealt with one dead person before; that was some time ago, not a nice job. I move slowly into the bedroom. This room is again pitch black, I fumble my way around trying to find the light switch, finally click, the room is flooded with light. Fiona, Jean and Megan are stood in the doorway frozen, staring at the bed. I can almost hear my own heartbeat. There is a large lump under the eiderdown, the shape of a body, it doesn't appear to be moving. On the side table are an assortment of bottles containing medication, on the floor is an overturned bottle, a dozen or more tablets are strewn across the floor.

I walk across, my legs feel like jelly I quietly say, "Ethel, Ethel are you OK?" No response. I take a deep breath, and gently pull the cover down. The air is icy. I lean forward, no sign of breathing, her face is pale, her teeth are missing, which makes her look older, more vulnerable. My hand trembles as I slowly touch her shoulder, it is cold. Ethel's eyes are half closed. "Ethel, Ethel ", I whisper, gently shaking her shoulder.

Suddenly Ethel sit bolt upright, knocking me backwards and she shouts,

"Where's my bleeding hearing aid".

My heart stops then leaps into rhythm. Megan, Fiona and Jean all scream together. Ethel screams. Jean swears, Fiona thanks god and Megan laughs hysterically. I smile realising, Ethel isn't dead, she is very much alive and by the look on her face, not very pleased with our intrusion.

Ten minutes later Ethel is in her chair, with her blue fluffy dressing gown wrapped around her, teeth and hearing aids in place and a cup of tea in her hand. Jean and Fiona have returned to the office and the crossword puzzle. Megan looks embarrassed, as she apologises, "I'm so sorry Ethel, I was worried about you. We didn't mean to scare you."

"It's alright my love, I just had a bit too much of my liquid medication." Ethel gives a mischievous smile.

"Had a bit of a cold coming on so decided to have a nightcap, drop of whiskey. Seems to have done the trick I feel much better today." Ethel laughs.

We quickly tidy the kitchen. Megan makes Ethel a boiled egg, soldiers of bread and butter and another cup of tea. I collect the medication in the bedroom, most of it is prescribed or pain killers. Ethel had taken her regular pain killers on top of whiskey and this had knocked her out. After her food Ethel decides she will go back to bed for an hour. The film club starts at three o clock and she wants to watch, because it's a Frank Sinatra film,

"He's a bit of alright him you know, met him once in Vegas. Always had a bit of glamour on his arm, gave me a twenty-dollar tip once. That were a lot of money then". Ethel grins.

As we leave the building Megan apologises to me,

"Sorry to have got you down here for nothing. Feel as though I overreacted and now Jean and Fiona are probably smirking in their office. Sorry"

"Don't be sorry, you did the right thing, better to be safe. I'm going to put a complaint in against Jean. It was her role to check Ethel was OK, you only see her once a week. Jean's attitude makes my blood boil. I do think we should make an appointment for Ethel to see her GP though, it's about time her medication is reviewed. I will organise that when I get back to the office. Thank you for caring Megan, Ethel did appreciate you raising the alarm, even if we did give her a bit of a shock!"

"I think I nearly died when she sat up!" Megan laughs, we both climb into our cars. Ethel waves from her bedroom window.

WHO CARES?

Third Visit

Chloe's Grandmother, Daisy, has agreed to see me, I arrange to call around on Thursday morning at ten o clock. Daisy explained that this was a good time, as her daughter and Chloe usually pop in then.

The house is set back, with a communal grass verge between the road and the pavement. Each house looks the same, built in the nineteen sixties, modern practical two bedroomed semis. Daisy's house looks well cared for, there are clean white blinds at the windows, dressed either side in peach and cream curtains. The garden is neat and full of flowers. I ring the doorbell, the door is opened by a large man, in his fifties, wearing a tee shirt and tracksuit bottoms. He stares at me then gruffly asks,

"Yeah, who are you?"

I feel extremely small, mainly because he is two steps off the ground, plus about a foot taller than me.

"Carla Saxon, Social Services. I have an appointment with Daisy Hardcastle". There is a slight tremor in my voice which I hope he doesn't notice.

"Mam, Mam, you are expecting someone from Social Services?" His hand is poised on the door as if ready to shut it in my face.

A large buxom lady, with platinum blonde hair piled on top, looks around the door. "You Carla?"

"Yes". I watch as the man releases the door and returns back into the house.

"Just ignore him, he's been on the night shift so he's grumpy as hell. Barks worse than his bite mind". Daisy is wearing a pink floral housecoat, which finishes just above her knee, with black furry mules. Inside the living room is cosy, not what I expected, it is clean, modern with bright cream and peach décor, matching cream sofas against two of the walls. In one corner is a small machine with pipes coming out of it.

"That's mine", Daisy offers "Bloody compressor nebuliser, bit unsightly isn't it. Does the job though. Can't get my breath, usually worse in the mornings. Always had asthma as a kid, now diagnosed with COPD. Cup of tea then?" She heads towards the kitchen, looking over her shoulder she calls, "Take a seat. Keith, do you want a cuppa I'm just making one". I hear a faint call of No, from somewhere out the back.

Daisy brings the tea in a teapot, two mugs, milk jug and sweeteners. "So, you want to talk about our Chloe, do you? Bit of a handful she is. You have milk? Sweeteners?" I nod to all three questions.

"Yes. I'm a bit concerned that Chloe has nowhere to sleep, she is sleeping around on friend's sofas. She missed her benefits payment this week. Which means she probably has no money". I try to appeal to Daisy's conscience.

"Well I hope you aren't expecting me to take her in? I can tell you a few things about that cheeky little monkey". Daisy passes me a mug of dark steaming tea. Daisy sits back in her chair and starts to describe Chloe, although a lot is very negative, I can sense there is some real affection for Chloe underneath. "I've had her living with me since she was three months old, our Pam had a hard time at the birth, then suffered with post-natal depression, terrible that was, started about a month after Chloe was born. Pam wouldn't get up in a morning, always tired. Then sleeping during the day. Cried a lot too. Refused to feed Chloe, so I had to step in. Chloe lived here with me. It weren't ideal. Then Pam goes and gets herself a new man, that was it then, Chloe hardly saw her for over a year."

"Sorry, what about Chloe's Dad? Where was he?" I was curious.

"Well, there's the thing. He got sent down, five years for armed robbery. Daft Beggar got in with the wrong crowd. He were the driver, they tried to rob a Petrol Station. Trouble was they turned up two hours after the security van had been and removed all the cash. There was only a fifty quid float. One of them got clever and started to smash the place up with a car iron. The young lad serving tried to stop him and got sixteen stitches in his skull for his trouble." Daisy starts to wheeze, she reaches for her nebuliser, after a couple of minutes she continues. "Chloe has never met him. Thought it best if he is gone, so, well, thing is she thinks he's dead. We never corrected her on that. Didn't seem much point. Chloe was always into mischief, put next door's cat in the washing machine, emptied a bucket of worms into her teacher's handbag, painted her bedroom once, with lipstick, felt pens and jam. That were a bloody mess I can tell you. Mostly, kid's stuff. Then as she grew older, she started to hang around with girls two and three years older than her. You've seen she is quite mature looking, always had a good figure.

First it was shop lifting, I kept finding things in her bedroom."

"What sort of things?" I didn't see what difference this would make but I was curious.

"Oh, bits of make -up, sweets, chocolate, odd bits of costume jewellery. Always had an excuse mind. Such a body gave it me; I'm just looking after it, I borrowed it. Answer for everything that girl." Daisy smiles and sips her tea.

"Then she started staying out till all hours, bad mouthed me when I checked up on her, you wouldn't believe some of the language that girl uses. Police brought her home twice, she had been thrown out of a night club, got a warning for shouting and swearing at the police. Fortunately, she hadn't been drinking. She was always in trouble at school, got excluded on a daily basis. Refused to go into lessons, swore at teachers, fighting with other girls, wrote "The Headmaster is a Wanker" in black paint, not sure where she got the paint? All over the wall outside the main entrance!! I ask you!! She even put her initials on it, in case

131

there was any doubt. Then our Pam took her back full time, it was affecting my health, I had to go in hospital, and it seemed appropriate for her to go home.

Up until then Pam had her three days a week. It just went from bad to worse. Chloe never liked any of the men Pam saw. Our Pam has never been strong, always needed a man. Unfortunately, she doesn't have a lot of luck with them. Think there have been four in her life since Chloe was born. Lot of time wasters if you ask me. So, then Chloe gets pregnant, of all the things!! She can't look after herself let alone a baby."

The doorbell rings, I watch as Daisy struggles to get up and answer the door. "Hi Mam". It is Pam, Chloe's mum. My first impression is that Pam isn't old enough to have a daughter as old as Chloe, let alone be a Grandmother. Pam is petite, about five feet two inches. My Grandmother would have said, 'she weighs not more than seven stone wet through'. Pam is dark, short hair cut in layers; a pixie cut. Pam looks nervous, almost frightened. Daisy explains the purpose of my visit. Pam responds, "Well, I can't have her, Phil won't have her in the house again. Not after what she did last time. There's no way Mam". Pam addresses her mother, avoiding eye contact with me.

I formally introduced myself, then ask, "Who is Phil? And what has Chloe done to upset him?"

"The little bitch took fifty quid out of his wallet. I knew it were her, who else could it have been? She denied it of course. Then told me she had seen him in the pub with that Susan Kershaw down the road. Phil was furious, she is such a little liar, always trying to cause trouble." Pam is now red in the face, emotions bubbling over, "No way I want her. She let them take that baby away too, what sort of mother does that?? What sort of bitch puts a baby at risk like that?" She is now physically shaking. "Mam, I can't have her. She will have to go somewhere else; he'll kill me if I take her back in".

I try to calm the situation. "At the moment I am here to

investigate options. Chloe is still a minor. Chloe is vulnerable and I do believe, Chloe deeply regrets what happened with James. I want what is best for Chloe, I am looking into residential care homes but to be honest they are not always the best solution. We always try to see if a member of the family can help first. Of course, there is also Foster care, these days there are lots of younger children in need of this service, the chances are that Chloe would be eighteen before a place was found. Then she is considered an adult."

"Well, I've said what I think. She isn't coming to me". Pam folds her arms in resolution.

"Wouldn't come to you if it was the last fucking place on earth. Especially with that Dickhead there!!" Chloe enters from the kitchen. I wonder how much she heard.

All three, mother, daughter and Granddaughter start to shout at once, each voice overlapping. Like some sort of tribal ritual each one states their views slightly louder than the other. Then in comes Keith, his voice booming out, drowning the others "Will you all Shut the fuck up!!!"

Daisy rolls her eyes to the ceiling and plonks down into her chair. Pam takes a tissue from her pocket and sniffs into it. Chloe stands with hands on hips staring at me, her expression is thunderous as she spits, "Well what did you think would happen?"

Pam storms out, Chloe shouts after her "That's it run away, go back to the creep. You don't care about anybody, you're a selfish bitch".

Daisy looks exhausted, she leans back in her chair, pulling her mask over her mouth. Chloe is angry but there are tears of hurt behind the anger. Chloe turns to me, "See, I told you this was a waste of time. They don't fucking want me, I'm bad news". With that Chloe runs out.

Keith speaks, less forcefully, "Why do you put up with this Mam, you don't need all this drama, just tell them all to piss off". Daisy shakes her head in defeat. Keith shrugs, he's obviously seen this played out many times, lighting a cigarette he goes back to the kitchen.

"Sorry about this Daisy, I have to try family first. Chloe is still very vulnerable". I am feeling a little angry and despondent about how the situation developed, Chloe is probably very upset now. "I think maybe I should go after Chloe?" I pick up my bag.

Daisy removes the mask and sighs, "Waste of time, she will be long gone. I know that she is vulnerable, I will have to have a quiet chat with Keith, or maybe my other daughter Angela can help, she has before. Her husbands is a bit difficult about letting Chloe stay. Leave it with me. Don't bank on a happy ending though. Chloe has caused a lot of upset in this family." Daisy is upset, I feel these family disputes occur too often and Daisy pays the price with her health.

As I leave for the office, I scan the streets for Chloe. She must be hurting; did she hear everything that was said? No child needs this sort of negativity. I am sure Chloe's behaviour over the years has been bad; maybe for a reason, a deep-down hurt inside her. Feelings of rejection, unwanted, unloved, passed around the family. Who did she have to talk to? I would try to call her upon my return to the office.

An hour later I ring Chloe's mobile, after the fifth ring she answers. "Yeah?" I not sure what to say. "Hi Chloe, I wondered if you'd like to come for a burger and fries with me?" the line goes quiet. "When?" Chloe asks. "Now if you are hungry, I can meet you on the corner of Crescent Road in about fifteen minutes, how does that sound?". I needed to get lunch, might as well make it a working lunch I smiled. "OK". The line went dead.

Chloe is waiting on the corner, same rucksack over her shoulder, she smiles as I get out of the car. "Smart car that, how old were you when you learnt to drive?" Chloe is walking around the car, looking at the pile of papers on my back seat and my discarded water bottles. Note to self, clean car this weekend.

"Oh, I was twenty years old, I had a small blue fiat, my first ever car" I grin. We walk together to the counter. "What would you like?" Chloe studies the menu board then says with confidence, "Big Mac, Fries, Coke and apple pie. Please."

I order the food and we select a seat near the window. Chloe obviously hasn't eaten for a while and the burger disappears, almost before I had finish unwrapping mine. "Hungry?" I ask. Chloe nods and starts eating her fries.

"Sorry about the meeting at your Grandmother's, that wasn't how it was supposed to be". I watch Chloe as she raises her eyes to the ceiling.

"That OK, I know what they are like. My Grans OK usually, but the others don't like me much. Bet my Gran said no didn't she, she won't go against Keith and Pam, they don't want me there." Chloe fills her mouth with fries.

"Well, not exactly no, your Gran said she would talk to the others and maybe ask Angela if she can help out, she did help you before, didn't she? Maybe you can go and stay with Angela again?" I watch Chloe's expression change, is it fear or panic flashes across her face?

"No, no I can't stay at Angela's he wouldn't like it. He gets really mad if he thinks I've been there, we have to be careful, he's a mean bastard. He hits her you know. Nasty git, I hate him. Anyway, Angela won't let me stay there." Chloe's emotions are really high, I feel as though I have somehow hit a very sensitive nerve.

"You get along with your Aunt though, Angela? Do you think it's worth talking to her?" I am grasping at straws.

"No, she is scared of him, her partner, they're not married, she

135

lives with Ron. They've been together for five years he works away a lot, drives a lorry. Likes to drink when he's at home. What is it with the women in my family always seem to get the nutcases, the psychos? That Phil, Pam's with now, he's a bad one. I saw him with someone else in the pub, when I asked him about it, he denied it, said Pam would never take my word against his. Then he told Pam I nicked his fifty quid, lying bastard, I never touched his money. Course Pam believed him, I tried to tell her what a fucking liar he is, but she wouldn't listen. So, I get thrown out, even Gran thinks I did it." Chloe screwed up the paper which had held her burger.

"This is why you have got to help me get somewhere decent to stay. My mate says I can stay two more nights on her sofa, then I have got to leave. She will get in trouble from her landlord if he thinks she has me staying, it's supposed to be a one bedroom flat. I need my own place then I can get James back. It's really important to me to get him back, you know, I'm all he's got, I'm his mum." Chloe stares into the paper cup of cola, sadly, then in a determined voice, "Right so what are you going to do next. Shall I come and see you tomorrow morning?" Chloe isn't giving up.

We agree to an afternoon appointment, at the office. I decided to try again the subject of Angela as a possible source of help. "So, do you think I would be wasting my time asking Angela then?"

"Yeah, definitely. It's him. He hates me. Told me to keep away or he'd kill me. Don't think he could, he usually too pissed to stand up. Still he has hurt Angela before. She lost a baby through him. Pig doesn't care about her really. He is a real pervert."

"Wow, Chloe, you really don't like him, do you? If he is so bad why does she stay with him?" I was trying to imagine what he had done to make Chloe so angry.

"She says she loves him, but she doesn't know about him, she doesn't understand what an evil bastard he is. I know what he's like, what he is capable of. I'd like to cut his balls off". Chloe's face is flushed, anger is pumping through her veins.

"That's a lot of hatred there Chloe, what could he have done to her that upset you so much? Did he hurt her in front of you?" I ask quietly.

"No. He hurt me. But I don't want to talk about it. I don't want to ever see that creep again. It's past now, don't want to think about the monster." Chloe sips her cola and continues, "Right, so I will see you later tomorrow, can we go for a Mac Ds again? I really enjoyed today. My mate has subbed me twenty quid, so I can treat you if you like". Chloe grabs her bag and pushes the apple pie inside. "For later". She beams.

"Chloe if he hurt you, we really need to talk about it, he might do it again. Can you tell me what happened, I promise not to do anything, if you don't want me too?" Chloe stands up, glaring at me for a second, she pushes her hair off her face, "No point, it's done with now. I have to get on with my life and look after James, he's the one good thing that exists in my life. See you". With that Chloe turns and walks out of the restaurant, she waves as she passes by the window.

Back in the office I am able to find a desk by the window, it is quiet, I can update my files, make some calls and try and find a placement for Chloe, if only for a few nights. I pull up Chloe's file on the screen. Chloe had been living with her Grandmother while she was at school, she was always in trouble, silly things, swearing in class, fighting with other girls, not attending lessons. Then she moved out and went to live with Angela and Ron, she was only with them for about three months, something happened, and she moved back to her mother's, Pam and Phillip her partner. That didn't last long, a few weeks later Chloe discovered she was pregnant. Chloe went back to her Grandmothers, she stayed at her Grandmothers until she gave birth.

During that time Social Services had been involved as Chloe was under-age, however, Chloe refused to say who the father was and insisted she wanted to continue full-term with the pregnancy. Chloe had a long and difficult birth and James was born prematurely at 35 weeks. He was very small and remained in hospital for two weeks to get his feeding programme established. Chloe went home but visited daily. Staff reported that Chloe's visits were consistent, Chloe attended at feeding times during the day, staff covered the night. Chloe was allowed to take James home to live at her Grandmother's house. Her Grandmother had agreed to support Chloe. After six months the relationship with her Grandmother broke down, Chloe was leaving James with her Grandmother, going out with her friends most evenings and at weekends, this led to scenes and arguments within the family.

There were money issues; Chloe was struggling to cope with her role as other, frequently leaving James crying, failing to change him when needed. Her Grandmother eventually reported this to Social services, her own health was deteriorating, and she couldn't cope with a baby and Chloe's behaviour. Chloe was still at school but refused to go. Chloe was given a support worker to visit and help her with the baby each day, things appeared to stabilise for a while. Then her Grandmother was taken ill, it was decided that Chloe couldn't stay there alone, her mother wouldn't take Chloe and the baby, Angela agreed to have them both stay with her and Ron. Chloe' freaked out' and ran off with James.

They stayed at various friends' houses, which was totally unsuitable. In the end, in desperation Chloe had taken the keys to her friend's car; wrapped herself and James in a sleeping bag and climbed into the car, intending to sleep there. Her friend reported Chloe to the police, they came and took both mother and baby in. James was placed in a foster home. Chloe was returned to Angela's house, where she stayed for one night, then went missing. It was believed she was sofa surfing at this point. During this period Chloe had been referred to the children's mental health team. School had reported seeing signs of self-harm on both her arms, Chloe had also arrived at school with her fringe uneven, as though some one had attacked it with a pair of blunt scissors, when staff enquired what had happened Chloe admitted she had try to cut it with nail scissors. This is often an early sign of self-harm, to cut hair in an almost aggressive way, to inflict hurt and embarrassment on oneself. When Chloe reached eighteen, she would be transferred from Children's services, to Adult Services. I was appointed to support my newly acquired little friend; it was now me she was looking to for help, I had to try.

The next three hours were spent on the telephone, trying to find somewhere for Chloe to stay. I tried Angela's number a few times, there was no reply. Finally, I found a place in a young person's hostel. It was a modern building in town. Staffed twenty- four seven, they had rooms for twelve young people. Everyone had their own bedroom and shared a communal lounge and kitchen. They were encouraged to be independent but had to abide by the rules. It sounded ideal, a vacancy had arisen that day, places were rarely available, there was a waiting list. I know Shelia, the senior manager, I ring her. As a favour she agrees to meet Chloe the following morning at ten thirty. I immediately get on the phone to Chloe and ask her to meet me at ten. Chloe doesn't seem too keen on the phone, saying she wants a flat, somewhere for her and James to stay. I convince her to at least come and see the hostel.

It is eight thirty when I arrive home, the house feels cold, I flick on the central heating, the kettle and the hot water for my shower. I look in the fridge, eggs or half a pre- packed salad from two days ago. I finally settle on a chicken madras with rice, ready meal for one from the freezer. I put the curry in the micro and go to have a quick shower. I wonder where Chloe is spending the night. I would hate to think of my daughter being out in the streets, staying wherever she could find a bed. So many children are now living on the streets, so many dysfunctional families. I hope that Chloe will give the hostel a chance, it is the best option for her. One other thing worries me, on the minutes of a review meeting with Chloe, the proposed adoption of James was discussed. Chloe had said she understood what adoption means. I'm not convinced that she does understand. Once James is adopted Chloe will lose all rights to see him, she currently sees him every week with his foster parents, she can take him presents, have photos with him, feed him, cuddle him. Chloe doesn't understand that adoption meant she would never see him again. I wasn't sure how I was going to handle this; it would have to be just one step at a time. First priority is to keep Chloe safe.

After my shower the phone rings. "Hi, how you are doing?" How did he manage to do that, Paul always rings when I need company? His voice always makes me melt. My voice changes, not consciously but somehow it becomes softy, quieter.

"Hi, what a nice surprise. I am just chilling on the sofa, been a busy day, You?"

Paul laughs "Well I just happen to have a nice bottle of red here, perfect for relaxing, I can even throw in some peanuts if I'm invited round".

"Ho, how can I resist, peanuts. See you soon". I put the phone down and dash upstairs to change out of my fleecy pyjamas and bed socks into some casual jogging pants and an oversized, off the shoulder tee shirt. I glance in the mirror, 'who says you can't look sexy at forty, not bad girl' I muse to myself. I switch the lamps on and some soft music just right for chilling.

Fourth Visit.

"Do you know what it feels like to hurt so much that you can't even cry?" Chloe stares at me across the desk in the office, she is still holding her rucksack in front of her, clinging to it as though it contains her entire life. Chloe looks tired, she hasn't her usual sparkle. There is no lipstick today, no rosy cheeks. Just a little girl who has lost something.

"I'm not sure what you mean Chloe, has something happened?" I'm worried.

"You hurt so much, that it's a pain in your chest, a hollow sort of pain, you feel like you can't breathe. You can't get your head sorted; it's just flooded with words". Chloe leans back in the chair and stares up at the ceiling.

"You want to feel the pain, but you are numb, something in the hurt has switched off from the pain, bit like watching a video. I want to feel the pain that's tying me up in knots, I can't. Even this doesn't work." Chloe's eyes meet mine as she pulled up her sleeve, there are three long gashes along her arm between her elbow and her wrist. They looked angry red and quite deep, not deep enough to require stitches but severe enough to cause infection. Chloe watches my face, seeking a reaction.

"Oh, Chloe why didn't you call me, you don't need to be alone with all this hurt. Will you at least let me clean up the wounds?" I want to reach over and hug this little girl who had already had so much rejection in her life. Chloe murmurs, "If you want to."

Twenty minutes later the wounds are clean, we sit on the sofa drinking hot chocolate. Chloe winced when the antiseptic touched the wounds, she stoically remained silent, until I offer her hot chocolate.

"Do you want to talk about the hurt that made you cut yourself?" I saw Chloe's eyes flick around the room, then settle on the floor in front of her.

"It's just a big mess isn't it; my life is Shit. Some people have good lives, happy families, not me. I get the bloody Adam's Family, freaks. It just goes on and on, no point in talking about it. Life just keeps throwing shit at me."

141

I smile at Chloe; she is definitely on a downer. "Can I tell you a story that helps me when I feel low?" I watch her resigned look, ready for another grown up lecture. "OK then, but I've got to go in a minute".

"Good, this is a short story, about a farmer who had a donkey, the donkey worked very hard for the farmer, carrying his things every day. Then one day the Farmer decided he didn't need the donkey any more, so he threw the donkey down a deep well". Chloe looked across at me "What's this got to do with me?" I smile, "Well the donkey was down the hole and couldn't see a way out, everything was black. The next day a villager came by and he threw too large sacks of rubbish down the well. Later another boy came; he threw four old tyres down the well. The following day lots of other villagers came and threw their rubbish down the well. The donkey had to keep standing on the rubbish, so he didn't get buried. After the fourth day the donkey climbed out of the well. The moral of this story is no matter how much shit life throws at you, you have two choices. Let yourself be buried by it or use it to build you up and get you out and back on track". Chloe registers the story, she then nods her head "I get it, I get it, I am the donkey, right? If people give me shit, it should make me stronger". I laugh, "Well. Yes, sort of. We all have bad experiences and we need to use them to make us better, stronger people." Chloe drains her cup., standing up, she says, "So, what are we going to do about this hostel then?"

I explain to Chloe about the hostel, how it operates. At first her response appears negative, until I mention that boys are also accommodated there. I ring the hostel and confirmed our arrival at ten thirty. Chloe chats on all through the journey across town, she had stayed at a boy's house last night, but it was very dirty, he had loads of people there, so she didn't get much sleep because they were talking nearly all night. When we pulled into the car park Chloe says, "I always wondered what this place was, I thought it was some kind of posh kid's school."

Once inside Shelia greets us, Shelia has a great attitude

with young people relaxed but firm, always seems to have things under control. Shelia dresses for the part in jeans, tee shirt and trainers. All the staff are casual, so much so that it's hard to tell some of the staff from residents. Chloe is extremely quiet, polite and seems intent on giving the right image, shoulders back, her most innocent smile, yes please, no thank you. So much so that I wonder if the real Chloe has left the building. Sheila shows Chloe a room should she be offered a place. It is a bright, airy single bedroom with a single bed, wardrobe, chest of drawers and a small desk with a reading lamp. Chloe asks, "Don't we get a TV?" Sheila smiles, "You are welcome to bring your own if you have one. Most people prefer to watch TV in the lounge, we have SKY and Freeview there, plus a selection of games and DVDs". Chloe nods, trying not to show how impressed she really is, I know this is luxury compared to where she has been staying over the last two years. Shelia then introduces us to three residents, two older boys who are busy on a games console, they both stop and say hello, the blonde one of the two, who is extremely handsome looks at Chloe and asks, "You coming to stay here then?" Chloe's face turns bright red, "Err, Yeah I think so." Chloe glances at Shelia then at me. Back in the office, Sheila explains she had to clear any offer of a place with the other two manager's, whom she would see at a meeting the next morning. Sheila will telephone me with the decision. If successful Chloe could move in tomorrow morning. We thank Shelia and go back to the car.

"I think it might be alright there, they won't want me though when they find out what trouble I've been in. What about my arms? Do they know I have a baby?" Chloe is determined this place will not be available.

"Sheila knows you have a baby and has access to your file. None of the residents will know anything about you. It's up to you who and what you tell." I reassure her.

Back at the office we agreed that Chloe will return tomorrow morning to find out the result. Chloe leaves with a head full of self-doubt. It's hard for her to believe that things can go right sometimes.

After lunch I receive a call from Chloe's Aunt, Angela. She explains that whilst she wants to help Chloe, she can't, she had two young children to think about and Chloe is trouble. Besides which, her partner doesn't want her there and they can't afford to have another mouth to feed. I thank her for calling back; I feel relieved Chloe doesn't have to go back there, fingers crossed!!

Next morning, I await Chloe's arrival, by eleven o'clock Chloe hasn't rung, neither has Sheila. So I decided to stay calm and get on with writing a few e mails. At four forty-five my phone rings, it's Shelia, confirming the place is on offer for Chloe; we need to go in and deal with the paperwork, Chloe can move in once this is complete. I thank Shelia and make the excuse that I am very busy and will have to bring Chloe around the following morning. We exchange friendly chatter, busy as always, both drowning in paperwork. I like Shelia she is a genuine person, looking out for the young people in her care.

I then start to try and find Chloe, what is she doing? I ring her mobile, I ring her mother, grandmother and aunt no one had seen her all day, no one appears particularly worried. I have addresses and numbers for two of Chloe's friends. The first is Charlotte, she says she hasn't seen Chloe in nearly two years, she didn't want to ever see her again, she was very angry with Chloe who had apparently stayed at Charlotte's house and left the room in a mess, also stole a bag of food as she left. Charlotte's mother had been very upset. The second 'friend' Mel had seen Chloe the day before in the Town centre, she said Chloe was with a group of five or six young people, they were messing around and acting stupid, so she hadn't spoken to Chloe. Mel said they were in her opinion very childish and not the sort of people she wanted to spend time with. I ask if she might have any idea where Chloe would be, "Nah, she is a bit weird, always on her own, Chloe's hard work if you know what I mean? Did you try Angie's her aunty? Chloe was always going there when things went wrong."

By six o clock I am still no wiser, with Chloe's

background of chaotic behaviour, I wrestle with the idea of calling the Police. Just as I am going to, the phone rings, it's Daisy, Chloe's grandmother. Chloe had phoned her and asked if she can borrow forty pound to go out with her mates. When Daisy said no, Chloe shouted abusively down the phone, then the line went dead. So, Chloe was with friends, she had phone credit but obviously didn't want to be contacted. I pack my things away and head for home, it has been a long day.

Later I lie staring at the TV screen, I'm not really watching or listening my mind is replaying the events of the day, 'Did I know what it was like to hurt so much that you can't even cry?'

Yes. We had been trying for a child for almost two years, I already had a son, now we wanted a child that belonged to both of us. Then a routine visit to the doctor's discovered I had Endometriosis, with severe bleeding and discharge, this long-term condition can be serious and may cause difficulties in fertility. A smear test revealed abnormal cells, the word cancer was mentioned. An appointment was made for me to attend hospital for a biopsy. Thoughts of pregnancy were overtaken by thoughts of cancer. I went in for the tests, lying waiting after my pre-medical check, I wondered why everyone appeared to be going ahead of me. After lunch the consultant came to see me.

"Good afternoon, Mrs Saxon, may I call you Carla?" I nod agreement, why was he here?

"My name is Mr Forman, I'm the person who was going to conduct your biopsy. I'm afraid we have identified a problem in your pre-medical check. Have you ever had and problems with your heart?" He was now looking at my file, I shook my head, no one had ever mentioned my heart before.

"Well, the Registrar who did your ECG to check your heart. He's a very bright young man. He identified a definite problem; it appears you have a heart disease." He paused as I tried too take in the information. "Are you alright Carla? Do you understand what I have said?" He seems to be sat a million miles away, not talking to me.

I nod my head and smile, "You said I have Heart Disease, is that as well as possible Cancer?" I start to laugh, I know its nerves but how ironic is that, go in for one thing come out with two!! He stares at me; I can see my laughter is not the response he was expecting.

"Oh, well I will have to delay the biopsy, but I will send you for further tests and treatment to ensure we are on top of the situation. With regards to your heart I will refer you to a Cardiologist. We are very fortunate to have one of the best located about fifteen miles from here, Mr Blackmore, he will be able to give you more information and decide what action needs to be taken." He closes my file. I still have a stupid grin, it's all very surreal.

One week later I'm receiving laser treatment to burn off the abnormal cells. A week after I receive my appointment for the Cardiologist. A week after that I discover I am two months pregnant. A complete surprise, especially as I have lost nearly two stone in weight, which I had put down to stress. The Cardiologist and Obstetrician ask if I want the baby? Of course, I do, they are very concerned about my health, I am determined.

Five months later I am admitted into the hospital to be monitored, I am tired, low blood pressure, other than that fine, I have worked until my sixth month. Baby isn't due for six weeks yet. She arrives early, relatively painless for me, my daughter arrives weighing four pound six ounces. She is transferred to an incubator, just as a precaution. Two days later we take her home, she feeds well, sleeps well and proceeds to gain weight at an amazing rate. We are very fortunate. After the sixth month I am pottering around the nursery, tidying things, I stoop down to pick up a teddy bear. My husband is behind me, I try to speak, I can't, my words won't form, I drool saliva, I attempt to speak, words won't come, just some weird gargling noise. I see panic on Martin's face. I cry. He picks up the phone. I'm scared. Then my words come, quickly, garbled at first then more clearly. Martin puts the phone down. "What was that?" I ask, Martin is as bemused as I am.

The Doctor says my little episode is nothing to worry about. When I bent down to pick something up, I momentarily cut off the blood supply to my brain, which affected my Speech centre. It sounded very simplistic. It was probably the first real sign that my heart disease could be a condition with more severe consequences.

The last thing I expected. Ten months later, I am expecting again. It's too soon, it wasn't planned, my health is still uncertain, I have medication and regular tests. It appears I have something called Hypertrophic Cardiomyopathy, known in layman's terms as 'Sudden Death Syndrome'. Medical advice is that the pregnancy should not go ahead.

The need to decide has to be quick because I am estimated to be twenty weeks pregnant. I didn't understand the implications of this. I could think about it overnight, I would call in the morning. I confirmed our decision, it would ultimately be my decision, Martin had said. It was then arranged for my admittance into hospital. I was scared. Would it hurt? Would I be damaged? I would be alone, Martin had to care for Amanda. Once I was admitted Martin left. I was put in a bed on a medical ward. A doctor came to see me, he was very official, asked if I still wanted to go ahead, I nodded. He then explained that because I was twenty weeks into pregnancy, the termination would be done by the use of drugs, which would put my body into labour, I would go through an induced labour. I could have some help with the pain if needed. The process would start that evening. No one spoke to me on the ward, the nurses came, did what they had to do, but remained silent, the looks they gave me told me they didn't approve. Abortion is not an easy thing to accept, whatever the reason.

During the night I was in severe pain, no one came, I never cried out. told myself this was my punishment for what I was doing. It was too late to stop it, the minutes turned to hours, every few minutes I had pains which wrenched at my insides, Was I going to die, maybe this was my punishment. It hurt so much I wanted it to be over. In the early hours of the morning I felt water released from my body. I called the nurse. She looked at me and said it was nearly time, she came back a few minutes later, drew the curtains around the bed and presented me with a bedpan. Still reeling with pain, the bed pan was slipped underneath me. A final excruciating pain and I felt the baby leaves my body. The nurse lifted the pan and covered it with paper. My baby? Suddenly I had an urge to see this baby, my dead baby. I asked could I see it. I stared into the container.

That was the moment I hurt so much I couldn't cry, I couldn't breathe, I couldn't speak, I couldn't think. What had I done? I looked at the nurse, maybe she thought I wanted sympathy? She covered the pan and said, "it's too late now", she turned and walked away. That image of my child, upon reflection I believe it was a boy, my dead baby's tiny curled up body, with little hands, tiny feet. All his facial features intact, everything was perfect, except I had killed him. I had murdered a sweet, perfect baby. The image never goes away, I can bury it in my head, move on, but I can never forgive myself, I can never forget.

Yes, I did have an idea of what Chloe was going through, it was going to get a lot harder before she could move on, forgive herself. When James was finally adopted then Chloe would have to say Goodbye to her little baby, she would at least have the knowledge that he was alive, in a good home, who knows one day he might even come looking for his mother. These were the positives she would have to cling on to.

The next morning, I tried Chloe's phone before I left for the office. It was switched off. When I arrived at the office I tried again without success. There was no point in putting things off, I would give her till ten thirty, if Chloe hadn't arrived, I would ring Sheila and be honest about the situation. At ten fifteen I received a call from the local Hospital, the Nurse introduced herself and asked me if I knew a Chloe McCann. I said that I did, that I was her support worker. My mind was racing, what had happened? The nurse said that Chloe had been admitted last evening, she was unconscious on arrival. My name had been given to staff that morning by Chloe, listing me as next of kin. The nurse asked if I could attend the hospital, I agreed to be there in fifteen minutes. I found I was more upset than I realised, a stranger who I hardly knew needed me. I went to see Bill the manager, I couldn't tell him much, I was very upset, I didn't know how she was doing, what had happened, I just knew she needed me, and I had to be there for her. Bill agreed.

At the hospital I located the ward, the Nurse thanked me for coming and asked me to confirm my identity. We then went to see Chloe, she was asleep, looking closer to ten years old than seventeen. Wearing a hospital gown, she looked pale, her hair hung limp around her face. For the first time I saw the young, innocent child.

'What happened?' I ask the nurse.

Chloe had been brought in by ambulance around ten thirty last evening, she had collapsed in the town centre. The 'friends' she was with had apparently run off when she collapsed. A passer-by tried to help and phoned for the ambulance. She had woken briefly in the early hours and been able to tell staff her name and give my name as next of kin. Chloe had said someone had tried to poison her. Blood tests had shown that Chloe had taken drugs, possibly her drink had been spiked. Her symptoms suggested it was a drug often referred to as the Date Rape drug, Gamma-hydroxybutyric (GHB). Mixed with alcohol, probably on and empty stomach Chloe's body couldn't handle it, she lost consciousness. It was fortunate that someone helped her immediately or it could have been extremely dangerous. 'Did Chloe have a history of drugs?' the Nurse asks.

"No, nothing, not even alcohol or smoking". On this my reply was positive. "Some friends eh? Just leaving her'". I look at Chloe, so alone, so scared. How hard must it be to list your next of kin as someone you have only known a few days.

An hour or so later Chloe wakes, she appears genuinely pleased to see me. Chloe doesn't recall anything about the previous evening, two girlfriends had taken her to a public bar, there were some boys, she didn't know them, she couldn't remember having a drink. Chloe didn't know the full names of the girlfriends; they had met that evening in the bus station. None of Chloe's family had been informed, the hospital had stated they wanted to keep Chloe in for one night to observe she was clear of the drug. I stayed with Chloe for another hour and promised to collect her the next morning. I telephoned Shelia at the hostel, explained what had happened, Shelia was very understanding and agreed Chloe could join the hostel the next day. I then rang Chloe's Grandmother, explained what had happened and that Chloe was safe and well. Daisy didn't seem too surprised, perhaps after years of dealing with Chloe's misadventures this was nothing new. I said I would take Chloe to the hostel the next day.

Back at the office everyone was pleased to hear Chloe was alright and didn't seem to have any side effects from her involuntary drug intake. I wrote up my report on the day's activities.

WHO CARES?

Sixth Visit

I collect Chloe's bags from her Grandmothers at eleven then go straight to the hospital. Chloe is back to her normal self, sitting on the bed dressed in jeans and top from two nights ago. 'Where have you been? I've been waiting ages; they get up really early in here. Any chance of a burger on the way to the hostel?' Chloe rubs her tummy "I'm starving". She collects her rucksack and waves to the woman in the bed opposite.

Sheila welcomes Chloe to the hostel, there is paperwork to complete and a list of rules to be discussed. An hour later I leave Chloe settling into her new room, chattering away to a young girl of a similar age, about where the best place to go to have a manicure and acrylic nails done. I dared to breathe a sigh of relief; Chloe is finally in a place of safety where she will be cared for.

Over the following weeks I hear back from Sheila that Chloe is doing well, she has been looking at college courses and visiting her baby every week. Chloe is still convinced that she needs a place of her own to get James back. To this end we have a weekly visit, I try to explain the meaning of adoption, for some reason Chloe doesn't believe me, she is adamant that the lovely foster carers, the people who have James are going to continue caring for him until he can be with Chloe.

Then one wet Thursday afternoon, I had just finished my lunch when the receptionist announces I have a visitor, Chloe McCann. Chloe looks great, her hair is cut shorter in a new style with blonde streaks, she has make-up on and is dressed in a smart jacket and trousers, with complimentary blue blouse. 'Wow look at you all smart. Where have you been?' I am suitably impressed with the new look Chloe.

Chloe beams as she sits herself down on the sofa. 'You'll never guess, I have been out for lunch at the smart hotel just off the High St'.

'Really? You mean at the Grange? That's very expensive!!' I am puzzled.

'I know!!!' Chloe bubbles over; her news comes so fast I have difficulty following. Chloe has been with a Producer from the BBC, his team have taken her for lunch three times, in their big car, they had given her money and she had bought clothes. Yes, her Grandmother knew, her social worker knew, she was going to be famous. Chloe McCann was going to be a star of television, she would be famous, probably have to sign autographs. The film was about her and James, about him being fostered and that his foster parents wanted to adopt him, she had already done some filming with James at the park. Everything was fine, because she was now eighteen and could sign like and adult. Of course, Chloe's eighteenth birthday had been three weeks ago, she was now technically an adult.

Chloe left the office riding the wave of excitement, everything was new, she was bursting with ideas, confidence, there was nothing could stop this young woman.

I sit down to try and understand what is happening. I decided to ring her Social Worker and see what his view is. He doesn't seem too interested when I ask about Chloe, yes, he did know she is involved in a project to promote adoption, she is very keen to take part. Her family are aware and had said it is Chloe's decision. He is quite happy with the situation.

'But do you think Chloe understands what adoption will mean for her and James?' I ask, it is still my belief that Chloe doesn't understand.

'Yeah, yeah she likes the foster parents and is happy for them to look after James'. With that I am dismissed, he has clients waiting and a mountain of paperwork.

Just before five the telephone rings, its reception. "Hi Carla, I have a Miss Christine Cole on the line, wants to speak to you about Chloe Mc Cann". I have no idea who this is but ask for her to be put through.

"Hi, Carla speaking, how can I help?"

"Good afternoon Carla, my name is Chris Cole, from Loxley Solicitors Office, I understand that you support Chloe Mc Cann."

"Yes, that's correct". I am intrigued, what is this about?

"I represent Chloe in the adoption case. I have been meeting with Chloe for several weeks now, however, she came to see me earlier today, very excited, something about being on TV. Do you have any idea what its all about?" Chris speaks very formally, crisp and to the point.

"I only learned about it today from Chloe. I spoke to her Social Worker today; he says Chloe has agreed to make a film with the BBC about the adoption of her baby. I personally think it's a terrible idea and shouldn't be allowed even if she is eighteen now". I probably come across as some for of vigilante at this point.

"Why do you say that? Chloe did appear completely happy about everything."

One thing about my star sign is that we like to speak out, especially if we feel something is unjust, so I reply,

"Firstly, the film about the adoption of her baby, its my view that Chloe does not understand what adoption actually means, she thinks that everything will carry on as it is now, with access visits, gifts at holidays and birthdays. Secondly, I believe this is taking advantage of a young woman with a learning disability, a chaotic lifestyle and a history of self- harm. I think in the longer term this could do more harm than good for Chloe. Sorry but I feel very responsible for this young lady who has already undergone some major life changing experiences." My soap box speech is over.

"Would you be prepared to say that in court?" Chris enquires.

"Yes, of course. It's a form of abuse, taking advantage of a minor, she is eighteen but was assessed to have a learning age of nine years." The words had sprung from my mouth before I had even considered the consequences of what might follow.

"Just leave it with me, I will be in touch shortly. Thank you." With that Miss Cole was gone and I wondered what she might do.

One of the best things about the work are the range of weird and wonderful characters we meet each day. I am gazing at my computer screen I have no more visits this afternoon, this is very rare and I'm using the time to catch -up on notes and to book appointments for the coming month. My phone rings, it's Tony one of the Social Workers,

"Hi Carla, I have been delayed at this meeting, it's probably going to go on for another forty-five minutes. Would you be able to help me out? "Tony asks, he doesn't usually ask for help, so it must be something he can't put off.

" What is it you need?" I can visualise the relief on his face.

"I've got a client booked in for two, could you look after him till I arrive, give him a coffee, a magazine and apologise for my delay."

Doesn't sound too difficult, "OK". I agree. "Thank you, his name is Joseph Swan, he's a bit odd, should be fine, I'll be there as quick as I can. Been trying to see Joseph for two weeks so don't want to miss him, he's like the Scarlett Pimpernel. Thanks Carla, you are a star!" with that Tony hangs up.

Just after two o'clock the receptionist rings and says there is a gentleman to see Tony, I ask that Joseph to be shown into one of the interview rooms.

Five minutes later I enter the interview room. These rooms are informal, with armchairs and coffee tables, each room has facilities for making tea or coffee. This room has a large window looking out onto the street. In the room there is a man with his back to me staring out of the window, around six feet tall, slim build, grey hair, dressed in a smart suit, he turns around and smiles. He has a white shirt which looks new, a black tie, his trousers are neatly pressed, and his black shoes shine to reflect the surroundings. His teeth are perfectly white, a real toothpaste advert smile, he looks at me with piercing blue eyes.

"Good afternoon my names Carla." I am shocked, this man doesn't look like a client, he looks like he's on his way to a Directors Meeting.

He Smiles, taking something from his inside pocket, he points it at me, "Good afternoon, Bonds the name James Bond and I don't have time to hang around". I'm staring at him, is this a practical joke, is someone going to burst in and reveal hidden cameras. The man is deadly serious and blows down the barrel of the plastic but very realistic hand pistol.

I decide to act normal, "Can I offer you a coffee while you wait Mr Swan?" He immediately places the gun into what I can now see is a holster, "Bond, Bonds the name. Can't be too careful though, so perhaps better to use a fake name. Do you have any Martini?" I shake my head "Only coffee I'm afraid". He indicates that coffee will have to do. I am still a little wary of this man, I make him a coffee.

He drinks his coffee standing, he then asks me "Do you go to Follies Club on Tuesdays?" His question throws me, Follies is a nightclub and Tuesday nights I believe is for singles, not that I've ever been.

"Err, no I have never been to Follies." I answer. Follies is notorious for being a sort of female meat market, sex and one-night stands. Mr Bond shakes his head "Great pity that, I would have allowed you to join me for drinks there and maybe a bite to eat".

I find myself wondering how many women fall for his looks and his cheesy chat up lines and if they realise, James Bond is his alter ego personality. Just then the door opens and in walks Tony. "Thanks Carla, everything OK, managed to get away. Joseph, sorry to keep you waiting please take a seat." I say my goodbyes and leave.

An hour later Tony enters, winks at me and grins. "Bit of a character our Joseph isn't he."

"He certainly is, he could get himself into a lot of trouble, especially with that plastic pistol, its very realistic." I can see the funny side and smile.

"Oh, he does and frequently. Last week I got a call from the London Police, Joseph, or should I say James, took himself first class on the train to London, without paying. He then went to the House of Commons demanding to see 'M'. Of course, he was arrested and charged, for disturbing the peace, impersonating a Police Officer and for travelling without a ticket First Class on British Rail. I had to go and collect him. I doubt any of the charges will stick with his mental health issues, he's certainly a one off."

We laugh and joke, however, we both know that Joseph is exceptionally vulnerable. He appears confident, smart and has the 'chat'. He will be open to abuse and ridicule, he is a walking time-bomb.

WHO CARES?

Seventh Visit

Two days ago, I heard from Christine Cole the Solicitor, she wants me to take Chloe to a Psychologist who will ascertain if Chloe really understands what is happening about the adoption. Chloe has been very busy with her 'filming' commitments, she appears to be coping with all the attention, my concern is what happens to Chloe when the 'limelight' is switched off and there is no Baby James.

Chloe looked tired when she arrived, she seemed a bit subdued and I wondered if the appointment was worrying her.

"You alright Chloe, I will come with you to the appointment it should only take about half an hour. We can go for a coffee after if you like." I watched for the cheeky smile, but it wasn't forthcoming.

"Why do I have to see a stupid Psychiatrist, anyway, do they think I'm crazy?" Chloe asks.

"Not at all, it's a Psychologist, he is just going to talk to you about James, to make sure you know what is going to happen in the next few weeks. I'll be there if you need me." I wasn't allowed in the actual room, but I would be there waiting outside.

Chloe was in the interview for twenty minutes; she came out smiling.

"Wow, he was weird. Kept asking me random questions, Did I know who the Prime Minister is? How the hell would I know that. I asked him if he knew who the lead singer in Oasis is, he didn't. Then he asks if I think the foster carers will make a good mum and dad for James? Then a load more questions about James, He is really weird". Chloe was relieved to have completed the interview. We had a coffee and Chloe talked about the Hostel and how much she liked it there. She was thinking about training to be a Hairdresser, after things were sorted for James. Then she could afford to rent somewhere for them both.

At five o'clock I received a call from Chris Cole,

"Hello Carla, I have just heard back from the Psychologist, he confirms that Chloe does not have the mental capacity to fully understand what the adoption process involves and the consequences. I've set a hearing date for next Thursday afternoon. It will be in Manchester; I will send you the address and time. I will be there, with a Barrister, there will be a Judge and representatives from the Adoption Team, the BBC and Social Services." Chris made it sound so simple.

"Is it a court?" I ask naively.

"Not as such, but the outcome will be legally binding. This is more informal; it will be held in a conference room at a large hotel. Don't worry about it, you will be fully supported by our legal team, you know Chloe better than anyone so the Judge will listen to your views. I will see you there, if you need to bring anyone for moral support that's fine too." Chris sounded very confident. I decided then I would ask Bill my Manager to come with me, just for support.

I saw Bill the next day and explained about the hearing, I expected a lecture about getting too involved, instead he just said, "You did the right thing." Bill agreed to come for moral support, he had never actually met Chloe, but he was up to date with her case. The next few days were very difficult, I couldn't concentrate, the only thing in my mind was the hearing. Paul was very supportive, offering to drive me into Manchester for the hearing, I declined as Bill and I had agreed to go by train. I didn't see Chloe all week, but I spoke to her on the phone and she told me she had seen the film. I was surprised that it was finished, I asked Chloe what she thought of it.

"It's good, it does make me look a bit fat though. There is a nice bit in the park where I'm pushing James in his pram. It is mostly people talking about legal stuff and Social Workers. They said I might be able to have a copy after next week. They asked me if I was happy with it and I had to sign a piece of paper saying that I had seen it and liked it and understood it was for National TV. Imagine that, me on TV, wait till my mates see it.". Although Chloe sounded calm and relaxed, I could detect an undercurrent, maybe Chloe was starting to understand.

The Hearing

I felt strangely calm on the day of the hearing, Bill was waiting in the train station when I arrived. He looked different, he was wearing a suit and tie, I too had tried and wore my favourite navy blue suit, I used to call it my power suit, it cost a fortune but was nicely tailored, navy with a white shirt. Bill gave a low wolf whistle as I approached.

"Hey, look at you, dressed for business. How are you feeling? Nervous?". Bill smiled and touched my shoulder, "It's going to be fine." He looked more confident than he sounded. We didn't speak on the train, I mentally rehearsed what I was going to say for the millionth time. We got off the train and decided to walk to the hotel, Bill knew where it was, about fifteen minutes away, it was actually twenty minutes, but I wasn't counting. The four-star hotel was busy, we asked at reception which room the hearing with Loxley Solicitors was being held in, we were directed to the lower ground floor, room 10. The entire basement was a series of conference and meeting rooms, we could see people busy with flip charts and videos. We entered room ten, it had a small entrance foyer with tea and coffee available, through the glass doors I could see about twelve people standing around talking. My stomach started to somersault.

Once inside a small woman with glasses, dressed in a casual skirt and blouse walked over to us.

"Hello, Carla? I'm Chris from Loxley and this is the Barrister representing Chloe". Chris pointed to a tall slender woman, with a black trouser suit. Neither of the women were over thirty. We all took our seats. I counted fifteen people, each person was invited to introduce themselves, by a lady who announced she was the presiding Judge Keele. My hands were trembling under the table as the names and positions were announced, there were senior staff from the Children's Social Services, the Local Authority's Legal team, the Adoption and Fostering Services Director, the Film Director and Producer , the BBC's legal team, suddenly it was all too real. Bill looked at me and mouthed "OK?" I managed a small smile. First, we were all shown the Film. Then people were invited to speak about the film, about the process involved in choosing the location and the protocol followed to help Chloe through the process. They spoke at length of the benefits to the Adoption and Fostering service. The idea was to encourage people who foster to actually adopt, which I couldn't see any benefit in as foster carers have a different role to fill. An hour later I am sitting and listening, thinking everyone around this table believes this film is a great idea, apart from me and the Solicitor. Then the Judge asks me to speak. My knees are dancing under the table, I grip my hands to stop them shaking then I go on to automatic pilot. I give the speech I have rehearsed in my head a thousand times, Chloe's history, self-harming, dysfunctional family, single parent, chaotic lifestyle, her learning and physical issues. I charge in with both barrels loaded. Then I sit down, I don't know at when I stood up, but I remember pointing around the table asking "which of you will be there to pick up the pieces after all this is over".

That's it, I have probably just talked myself out of a job. The senior members of staff across the table glare at me. The Judge is speaking but its like my ears are stuffed with cotton wool.

".......and so, it is my opinion that anyone with an ounce of common sense could see that this entire scenario is completely unacceptable. The film should never have been made, I am therefore ruling that the film should never be shown on TV or any other media......"

It wasn't until Bill and I were outside that I realised the full implications, I had challenged the powers that be and actually won. The only thing that worried me now was how was Chloe going to take it.

CAROLE PARKER

Eighth Visit

I had booked a week's annual leave after the hearing, I needed time to relax, the stress of the case had affected me more than I cared to admit. Mr Tom and I spent two days in front of the TV watching rubbish. My daughter rang, my son rang, half the team rang, and Paul called in. Everyone wanted to say well done. I had a nagging feeling, what if I was wrong? What if this could have given Chloe a boost, made her more confident, helped with her healing process after James had gone. My doubts grew and no one could convince me.

When I returned to work it was with mixed feelings, I went through the motions, but I knew I had to see Chloe. I had tried to ring her; she wasn't answering her phone. Then on my third day back Chloe arrived unannounced.

"Hi, how are you? I called in last week, they said you were on leave?" Chloe looked relaxed; she was wearing striped leggings and an over-sized tee shirt.

"I'm fine. What about you? What about the film?" I ask tentatively.

"Oh, they decided to drop that, some technical reason. But guess what, they gave me two hundred pounds for the work I did!! How cool is that!! AND Sally and Rob the foster carers had a meeting with me and my Grandma, they said they are going to foster James long term. I can still see him and take him out. They said it will give me a chance to get my life in order, then when I am settled, and James is a bit older, he can come and stay with me. How cool is that?" Chloe is smiling from ear to ear.

"Wow, that is fantastic news. I am so pleased for you and James." I feel relief, things have worked out better than I could have imagined.

"Yeah, so I will stay at the hostel for a bit longer, its cool there. Now you can help me to fill some forms in for college, I'm going to be a Hairdresser. I'll come in tomorrow with them." Chloe is out of the door.

"Make it after two, I'm busy…" Did she hear me?

ALICE

"I don't think the human brain can comprehend the past and the future. They are both just illusions that can manipulate you into thinking there's some kind of change"

Bob Dylan

First Visit

I have several clients with dementia in various forms, with many degrees of severity. One lady lived in her own home alone. I was shocked when I first visited her to find notes written and posted all around the house. 'Switch the light off', 'make sure the backdoor is locked', 'Don't go outside', 'turn the tap off' and various other 'reminders'. However, she still went on walkabout a couple of times a week, the police brought her home, sometimes strangers would, and sometimes she found her own way home.

The Department had decided to try out a new, costly monitoring system, for a trial period, using technology. Cameras were fitted in the house, in her living room, kitchen and staircase. Alarms were set on the front and back door; these would raise the alarm at the office if she tried to go out. The family were also supplied with a computer linked to the system, so that they could monitor her safety. It isn't safe to lock a dementia sufferer in. The system had many flaws, several false alarm calls were made and often the lady was terrified, especially when staff arrived in the middle of the night, whilst she was in bed. Strangers with torches would enter her bedroom calling out her name. The lady wandered off one night, she was trying to get to her mother's house, her mother had passed away some forty years ago. As she wandered the streets in her nightie, staff arrived at the house, ten minutes after the alarm had sounded. Unfortunately, ten minutes was sufficient time for her to wander on to the main road. An unsuspecting off duty fireman was driving home from work, she walked in front of his car, the impact had killed her outright. The trial monitoring system was deemed a failure.

Alice is not a wanderer; Alice has frequent hallucinations. I witness this on my first visit. We have been for a walk to the shop, Alice has purchased some fresh vegetables and some fish for her supper. Alice likes to cook. I am helping her put the food away when she starts shouting, terrified she is standing in the kitchen staring at the microwave, telling someone to get out of her house. I stand behind her, there is no one there. To Alice it is real, she points her finger and wags it furiously at the microwave, shouting and threatening. I soon realise Alice is shouting at her own reflection in the glass. I ask Alice who it is, she replies its him again, I'm unsure who she is referring to. I ask her if I can try to get rid of him. Alice looks doubtful and slowly nods her head. I take a tea towel and place it over the door of the microwave. Alice relaxes almost immediately and thanks me for getting rid of him. Observing Alice over the next few weeks I notice the hallucinations occur mainly after dark, on any reflective surface, a mirror, a picture or a window. Alice is surrounded by her demons.

The main thing about working with dementia is having the ability to remain calm and resisting any arguing, correcting them may serve to aggravate the situation. Often family find this hard, when the person they know and love says something they disagree with, or something illogical or declare miss-information. It's more important to reassure and offer understanding. It's also important to be aware of the surroundings, in Alice's case her hallucinations are her reality, her surroundings are providing a stimulus by giving reflections. I often use distraction, especially when Alice is upset, talking about something mundane like the weather or food. Or a subject she likes to talk about, Alice was once a ballroom dancer and loves to reminisce.

Apparently, one morning staff found Alice sitting in the living room, very cold. Alice had taken her small electric fire and turned it over, so the heat elements and shiny reflective surface were flat against the carpeted floor, her tormentors hidden. Fortunately, as Alice had turned the fire over, she also pulled the plug out, so the carpet escaped with minor scorch marks. Nevertheless, this was a major risk factor and the fire had been removed.

Visit One year later

As she walked into the kitchen the cold air wrapped around her, a cloak of ice, penetrating through her body. Everything appeared as she remembered, the small table and chair against the wall, with the remains of her breakfast on the table, her cup of tea untouched, it would be cold now. The fridge and cooker against the other wall, with a tea towel carefully folded over the oven door. The clock above the shelf was ticking menacingly, had it always been so loud?

Slowly she forced herself to take another step into the room, he was here, she could sense his presence, he had returned again to torment her. Her pulse started to race; her heart pounded in her chest so hard she was sure he would hear it. Why had he come back? What did he want from her? Every time he came, he was more demanding, more controlling, more sinister. She knew that he was here waiting and watching, he had to be stopped. She had to take control, force him to leave, get him away from her home. She needed to be safe, it was her house, her kitchen, he had no right to be here. Her eyes slowly searched the room, he was there in the corner, lurking in the shadows his eyes watching, fixed, unblinking. He smiled a half smile, a smirk, a warning to let her know what he was capable of. He moved forward, sunlight from the window made it difficult to see him clearly but she could hear his breathing, rasping as though he was growling. Her hands started to tremble; beads of perspiration formed on her cold forehead.

Forcing herself to move she stepped forward, grasping the chair for support, she must not let him see she is afraid.

"What do you want? Get out of my house." She surprised herself with the force of her voice in the eerie silence.

"How did you get in? I told you I do not want you here. Get out".

He didn't move but the smile broadened mockingly, his eyes dark and cold cut into her, leaving every nerve in her body exposed. Fear mixed with hatred fuelled her temper.

"Get out, get out leave me alone, you are an evil man go away, I hate you, Get out of my house".

Her voice echoed around the room, still he stood silent and threatening in the corner. Suddenly, a noise came from the adjoining bathroom, she turned around, a young woman, with long hair and pale skin was coming from the bathroom. The girl stopped in the doorway. Her clothes looked dishevelled, as though she had been undressed, the girl laughed and pointed her finger at the man.

She knew instantly what had been going on, he had done this before, brought young girls into her house, he was dirty, disgusting. He used her house to have sex with these girls, she had seen him with them before. In her house, doing awful filthy sexual things with these girls who were brazen, unashamed. They were both laughing now pointing, staring, laughing, sneering at her.

"Get out. Get out. Get out of my house you dirty swine. Get this prostitute out of my house. Go away, get out, or I'll kill you both." Her anger made her chest tight; her breathing was difficult.

Summoning strength from within she grabbed her cup from the table, she lunged forward, throwing the cup of cold tea at him. The cup smashed against the wall; tea ran down leaving brown stains on the white paint.

He didn't move but she could see he was angry now, she had seen his temper before, her mind raced, she was trapped, how could she get away? There were two of them. Suddenly she felt the warm liquid trickle down her legs, she had lost control of her bladder, shame and humiliation were now mixed with her fear and panic.

A loud noise from the other room, a door closing? she turned quickly, were there others? Did he have another girl waiting was he planning to take more than one for his sexual gratification? It was the front door; she watched the door to the lounge. then sighed as another wave of fear and helplessness washed over her.

"I said Get out of my house. Dirty Bastard. Get out and take her with you!"

A voice called from the other room. She turns, the voice sounded faintly familiar. Glancing back only to see him and the girl scurrying out of the backdoor.

"Hello, Alice it's me Carla, just come to get you some dinner. Is everything OK?"

Alice turns around, her body is shaking. I remove my coat and step into the kitchen.

"Hello Alice, what's happened? is everything alright? you seem upset?"

"It's him, he's been back, he brought another girl in, I will kill him if he doesn't leave me alone". Alice is extremely anxious.

I glance around the room,

"Who Alice? who has been in? Alice did you let someone in?'

The small kitchen has nowhere for anyone to hide.

" Is there someone here? where are they?"

"No, they ran out the back door when they heard you come in".

I go to the back door it is locked from the inside, I turn the key open the door and look outside, there is no one there.

"Who was it? are you hurt? Who ever it was has gone now. "

Alice knew they may have gone now but they would be back, he always came back.

"He will come back." She mutters.

"Well they can't get back in now." I say as I look at the rear garden, it stretches down to the canal, there is a footpath along the canal side where people frequently walked their dogs, it is quiet today no one in sight.

"What happened to the wall Alice?" I ask.

"He threw my cup of tea at me, he's violent, dangerous" Alice smiles to herself, thinking how grateful she is that he has such a poor aim.

" Alice, I am very worried about this, I will have to report what has happened, we need to make sure you are safe, so no one can come into your home. Are you sure you didn't let anyone in?' I look at Alice, still wearing the clothes she had on yesterday when I visited.

Alice shakes her head,

"I NEVER, never let him in, or his women, he took a key when he came in last time, he said he would be back, he's evil".

'I think I need to contact the office, maybe your son? Alice." I am concerned, this is not the first time Alice has mentioned intruders, a common behaviour for people with dementia. Alice becomes extremely agitated and aggressive when her 'visitor' calls, she never puts a name to him. The upset causes Alice's blood pressure to rise, she sometimes has palpitations and issues with incontinence.

"They can't catch him he is too clever and if you tell my son, he will be angry and then he will punish me." Alice is starting to become agitated; shouting; she grips the chair till her knuckles are white,

"Please, you don't understand what he can do, please." Now Alice is crying, sobbing.

Tears start to trickle down Alice's cheeks, suddenly these give way to deep, heart wrenching sobs.

"Please, he scares me you don't know him like I do". Alice's fear is real.

I put an arm around Alice holding her close.

"You are safe, I won't do anything unless you want me to." I say this knowing I have no option but to report the incident. But for now, it is more important to keep Alice calm, especially as she has a pre-existing heart condition.

"Don't tell my son about him. My son will be angry. He's very busy my son and I don't want him worrying about this." Alice pleads through her sobs.

WHO CARES?

"It's alright Alice, I am going to make sure you are safe."

I clean up the spilled tea. Alice watches the backdoor, I see Alice is wet and help her change into clean underwear. I prepare a sandwich and a fresh pot of tea then sit with Alice. I complete the paperwork as Alice eats. This is only a twenty-minute call, not long enough to do everything that needs to be done, Alice is clearly upset, but I have another call in five minutes three miles away, there is no way I can get there on time in this traffic. Alice toys with the sandwich.

"I don't feel hungry, never liked ham on white bread, why do they always give me white bread?" she asked. I retrieve my coat from the sofa.

"Please Alice, finish your lunch, we will get you some brown bread if that's what you prefer. I will be back later to give you your tea. tonight, around four thirty, eat your dinner". I watch but Alice is deeply engrossed in pulling the ham off the bread. "Here is a yoghurt, strawberry and a biscuit. I know you like them", I watch as Alice opens the yoghurt and starts to eat, I'm pleased that at least she is eating something. The clock chimes twelve thirty, I should be at my next call. "Bye Alice, see you later". I call as I dash out of the door.

As I drive, I feel awful, poor Alice, the hallucinations are getting worse, more frequent and more upsetting for her. I must speak to Bill my manager when I get back, maybe the son can help. Though he wasn't very helpful last time we spoke, saying he has his family to consider and his work. I arrive at Hazlemere Road, only ten minutes late, Edna won't be pleased, she loves to have something to complain about.

Alice stands in the kitchen, then carefully placed the sandwich in the bin, concealing it under a paper bag, so they wouldn't go on at her about not eating. Alice returns to the lounge and waits She dozed on the sofa, there is a noise, a rustle, someone trying to get in. Was he back? Alice strains to hear; it is silent. Alice moves to the front window; it is starting to go dark already. Alice hates winter, she gets up in the dark and before long it is dark again. Some nights she has taken to sleeping on the sofa, just in case he comes back. This weekend Johnnie will visit, he is a good boy, works very hard. Since he married, how long ago had that been? two or three years? he had been more settled. Johnnie had moved with his wife Lucy to the seaside, Wales. Alice couldn't pronounce the name of the place. Alice took one of the family photos off the sideboard, she had been a beautiful bride, her and Johnnie looked so happy. There was another picture, this was Andrew or Stewart? she couldn't remember, lovely babies, she must ask Johnnie to bring them for a visit, Alice was sure Stewart would be starting school soon. Another photograph showed Alice when she was much younger, how old was she now? Alice remembered her retirement party, when she was sixty, did Joe her husband go to the party? Yes, she remembered they played the Anniversary Waltz and Joe took her round the dance floor, just like the old days, he had been a wonderful dancer, so light on his feet and so handsome. Alice lifted the image of her and Joe and gently kissed the picture.

"I still miss you my darling" Alice whispered softly.

Of course, Joe was very proud of the grandchildren, he had taken Stewart to watch the local football team, Stewart had laughed and made fun of Joe when the team lost six nil to a neighbouring team. Alice smiled as she recalled the gentle banter between the two. Stewart was working then, he had a good job, something to do with computers. Of course, it had been hard losing Joe, they had been together a long time. They only had one son, but Johnnie had been wonderful, such a good son. Always visited and always took her on outings, when he wasn't too busy with work; of course, he had a big new house now, and they went away on holiday a lot. Johnnie always sent her a card, there was one leaning against the picture frame.

'Greetings from Barbados.' Hi Mum, having a good time, weather very hot, food great, hotel beautiful. Working on the tan. Love Lucy and John.'

WHO CARES?

Alice carefully replaces the postcard. Johnnie would be due a visit soon, was it this weekend he said he had business over in Sheffield? he always stayed over with her when he had business, Alice liked to have him home it was like the old days, when he was at college, he was still messy though and she always had to tidy up when he left.

Alice froze as she heard a key turn in the lock, a female voice called out as the door opened.

"Alice, Good evening it's Carla again, sorry I'm running a bit late the traffic is terrible."

The young woman came into the room with a beaming smile.

I apologise for being late and sit down on the sofa next to Alice.

"Well, Alice how are you feeling now? Tell me what you've been doing this afternoon." I pat the sofa cushions into shape.

Alice watches me suspiciously.

"So, have you had any visitors today?" I ask.

Alice stares at me, "Who are you, do I know you?"

"Yes, I'm Carla I come here to help you prepare a meal, to make sure you are safe".

"Oh, No one has been today, not seen a single person all week. My son is coming at the weekend, I think he will bring Stewart". Alice appears to have forgotten the lunchtime incident.

"Oh that's lovely, what day is he coming? Saturday?' I ask.

Alice isn't sure, she looks puzzled, "Did he say Saturday?I think so." Alice replies.

"What did you have for lunch today?" I am aware that Alice

173

frequently doesn't eat the food prepared for her.

"Sandwich", Alice replied with confidence.

"Right shall we see what we have for your supper." I move into the kitchen and Alice follows dutifully behind. I read out the various options of lamb, beef, sausage and chicken dinners.

A chicken meal for one selected.

" Roast chicken dinner for one then?"

Alice nods.

"With apricot yoghurt to follow". I smile, as I read the instructions and place the tray in the microwave.

Alice starts to get her plate, knife, fork and her mug ready at the table.

Three minutes later the microwave pings, I empty the contents onto the plate. The food on the plate had nothing in common with the roast chicken dinner on the packet. Slices of potatoes pale and mis-shapen, a small piece of meat, which could have been pork or chicken and mixed vegetables. All coated with a grey coloured gravy. I ask Alice to sit down and proceed to make her a cup of tea. Alice moves the food around on her plate. I smile reassuringly, how else can we prepare a meal in the short time we have; I go into the other room. "Enjoy your meal Alice, let me know if you need anything else". I take down the logbook and fill in the notes for today's support.

Alice isn't sure what the ladies who visit write about or why they write in the blue book, they all spent time doing it. She watches as the woman scribbles on each page, her face deep in concentration. The woman took out a small plastic box, containing an assortment of tablets. They were sorted into little compartments. Alice knew these were tablets for blood pressure, cholesterol, vitamin D for healthy bones, anti- depressants, warfarin to thin the blood and memantine tablets to help with memory loss and confusion. Alice cannot understand who said she must take these, or why they thought she needed them. Alice is perfectly fit and healthy.

I know Alice had been diagnosed three years ago with Vascular dementia, the current average life expectancy for someone with this diagnosis, is five to eight years. Alice is now hallucinating more, in her confused state today's reality becomes mixed up with historical events, things from childhood, friends, family.

"Here are your tablets Alice, they need to be taken with food so have them now with your cup of tea".

I take the opportunity to look into the waste bin, sure enough there under the papers were the remains of Alice's lunchtime sandwich. I wait and watch as Alice takes her medication, then make a note on the file. Also noting that Alice has failed to eat lunch; she is now moving her supper around the plate with her fork but not actually eating.

Alice nods and makes to put a fork full of food into her mouth.

"Right Alice, are you alright now? is there anything else you need? Sorry but we are really short staffed today and I have four more calls before I finish. I am back on first thing in the morning so I will see you then. You have another lady coming at nine o'clock, to get you ready for bed and give you your cocoa.'

Alice smiles and nods, she has eaten half of the dinner and none of the yoghurt. I shout "Bye," reluctantly, I pull the front door shut. Time is our most precious commodity and we never have enough. As I sit in the car, I notice Alice in the window staring blankly into the dark, it's a long, lonely day for her. Maybe residential care would be in her best interest, her son had rejected

175

this, I suspect finance made a direct impact on his decision.

Alice looked at the meal, stood up and carefully scraped it back into the box before placing it in the bin. Alice washed her cutlery, plate and cup, placing the unopened yoghurt back into the fridge. The young people today really had no idea what proper food tasted like, it was all fast foods these days, plastic food as Joe used to say. Johnnie had once taken her into a Mac Douglas. Where they had been served with plastic bread rolls and rubberised meat. What on earth happened to home cooking. Alice smiled as she returned to her seat on the sofa. Maybe she could watch the news now? Alice pressed the button on the remote. It was already starting to go quiet outside, no traffic noises. Alice liked living here, it had always been her home. Alice remembered the day she moved in, what a performance that had been, she smiled to herself. Joe had hired a small van to fetch their belongings. It had broken down, he was so mad, it rained heavily, he was soaked to the skin when he arrived. He had walked five miles in the rain to get help from the garage. He was so angry. It wasn't Alice's fault; he was mad shouting and his eyes had been wild. Alice stopped she didn't want to think about that. Alice wondered if that was why they didn't have children. That lovely man, was he called Johnnie? Alice liked him, he came around to see her, thank goodness.

As I finish my last call, I decide to ring the office, I want to know if Bill will be in tomorrow, I need to speak with him. Sandra answers, she checks the whiteboard, "Bill has a meeting in town at nine but says he will be in for ten thirty". Sandra says efficiently.

"Great could you please leave a note that I would like to see him at eleven regarding Alice De Carlos. Thank you, see you tomorrow I'm signing off now". Last month we introduced a new monitoring system, so that the office had more information regarding visits, duration and time between each call. Staff now have to log in on arrival at the client's house, using the client's phone. The call is free, no charge to the client but many clients have difficulty understanding this. At the end of the visit staff then log out using the same method. Most staff regarded this as a management tool to 'spy' on staff, to check their whereabouts. Whilst staff resented the Big Brother approach, there was a general feeling that it could actually work to benefit staff as it would highlight how little time was allocated for visits, and travel between visits.

On my journey home I think about what I will say to Bill. Alice doesn't appear to be eating, she lives alone. Her son visits now and again, Alice has no other visitors other than staff doing their short meal calls, in and out, little time to chat, to get to know her. There have been issues with medication, Alice pretends to take the tablets then disposes of them when staff leave. Now staff have to stay and observe that the tablets are actually swallowed. There were too many like Alice , isolated in their own homes, it's often a very hard call for relatives, deciding what is best for a loved one. My daughter always jokingly says to me "You don't have to worry Mum, I will make sure you never have to go into a care home, I'll look after you". The truth is, life gets in the way, children have their own families to care for, care costs money, time, patience all take their toll.

I'm not surprised Alice isn't eating, the frozen dinners ordered by her son are pretty tasteless. The problem is staff just didn't have enough time to prepare a nourishing meal or to sit and ensure it is eaten. I have heard all the reasons why elderly relatives can't be supported by family. Costs, other family members take priority, accommodation, no space in the family home, work, time, other illness. We already have pets and father is allergic to rabbits and I really couldn't cope with incontinence. Yes, everyone has a valid reason, which doesn't help Alice. I feel frustrated, anxious, worried, and a little sad.

177

There was a low buzzing sound as Alice wakes, she rubs her arms and shivers, it is pitch black outside but for the faint orange glow of the street lamp. Alice let her eyes adjust to the darkness. A cup of tea, that will warm her. Alice shuffles into the kitchen still stiff from sleep. Before Alice switches the light on, her eyes see a shadow move outside the window. She freezes. Is it her imagination? She waits, nothing. Alice flicks the light switch. Moving to the backdoor she tries the handle it is locked. Alice, chastises herself, 'You silly old fool, what are you frightened of, your own shadow?' she smiles, then prepares a cup of tea, the time on the clock says three fifteen.

Not long now till it was time to get up, Alice liked to get up early, best time of the day Joe used to say, when the rest of the world is asleep. Alice returns to the sofa and pulls her old shawl around her shoulders, there is no heating on. Johnnie had arranged for the heating to come on early morning and early evening, for a couple of hours, that would be enough to keep the house warm, he had said. Alice shivers again and pulled her shawl tighter. Alice looks down at her feet, she was wearing an old pair of men's socks, Alice thinks they might have been Joes, she had found them in the bottom of her drawer, there was a tiny hole where her big toe peeped out, must darn that Alice mused, did she still have a needle? cotton? It was a while since she had sewn. Of course, when Johnnie was small, she would sew all her own curtains, make pillowcases, she had even mastered the art of knitting, Oh how Joe had laughed with her at her first attempt to make a jumper. She had misread the instructions and one arm had been six inches longer than the other. He had laughed, saying his arm would probably be longer one day, because Alice was so short, she constantly asked him to get things she couldn't reach. Alice at all of five foot laughed with him, his extra height had been useful, changing light bulbs, painting ceilings and lifting things into the loft.

Alice glances over to the pictures on the sideboard, Joe

hadn't been handsome, more sort of rugged, his skin was worn by the weather, having worked outside most of his life. He was strong, muscular with blue eyes that twinkled, his laughter was infectious. He was thoughtful, frequently brought her gifts and he idolised little Johnnie. Mind you he did have a temper, Alice didn't like it when Joe had been angry, he said cruel things, no she wouldn't think about that. Just remember the good times, Joe used to say get on with life, don't dwell on the past, let's have a little whiskey. He liked his whiskey did Joe. Maybe I should have a cup of tea now, to warm me up.

There is a sudden thud from the kitchen, Alice stands still another noise like something has fallen, maybe cats outside? Alice returns to the kitchen and stares out of the window there is a faint coating of frost on the ground, there it is again. Another more muffled sound this time it seems to be coming from Joe's shed. Was there someone there? Alice saw a cat run out of the shed door. No! The strays were forever going into the shed, they made it smell awful. Johnnie had said he'd fixed the door so they couldn't get in. He never did what she asked, he nodded agreement then did absolutely nothing, Alice knew he didn't believe her half the time.

Alice opens the backdoor and steps out into the cold night air, slowly, using the light from the kitchen window Alice approaches the shed. That is when she hears them. It is low at first just a mumbling, voices coming from inside the shed. Alice stops. It's him, he is back, she recognises his voice, he is with someone, a woman, they are whispering.

"Who's there"

Alice meant to be more demanding in her tone, but her voice came out trembling, like the rest of her body. Another thud, this time louder. Alice stumbles forward and her hand rests on the ice-cold garden wall. A black cat shoots past and leaps over the hedge. They are laughing now, laughing at her, they know she can hear them. Suddenly the door swings wide open she staggers back. Her foot slips on the frost; her legs disappear from beneath her. Alice hit her head on the stone wall and for a moment the pain sears through her body, causing her eyes to fill with tears. Alice lies in a crumpled heap on the ground. Alice can hardly breathe, her heart is racing, then she loses control of her bladder, the liquid feels warm against her legs. Slowly she pulls her legs towards her body and curls herself into a tight ball. Maybe he can't see her now? There is a noise from the house, the backdoor slams closed. Alice stares at the window. He is in the house, he is there smiling, holding a cup, mocking her, laughing and raising his cup, silently mouthing "Cheers."

The woman is with him, a blonde woman she puts her arms around him, whispering in his ear, they both laugh and wave to Alice. Alice feels the tears burning down her cheeks, yes, she knows him, she knows how cruel and heartless he is. He is a user, a womaniser, he is evil in its purest form. Alice hates him. The light in the kitchen blurs. the garden is shrouded in darkness, a cold deathlike blackness. Alice doesn't know where she is, it is cold, dark and very quiet. She can see a warm glow in the distance. "Help, help" she tires to call but her voice is just a whisper, it feels as though the wind had snatched her words and blown them beyond her reach. Slowly she crawls towards the light, there is no fear now just a strong determination to move toward the light, each movement, every inch brought severe pain, her breathing is loud and erratic, her heart pounding, the dampness of her lower body feels icy as her clothing sticks to her hips and legs. Alice pushes the wooden door it is open, she crawls inside, pushing the door closed with her feet. Then she stops, curls into a tight ball and let her eyes close, submitting to sheer exhaustion.

I am set to arrive at Alice's house at eight the following morning, Alice is the first call of the day, most of my calls don't normally start until eight thirty, Alice is an early riser. I drive round to the house and I'm surprised to see the lights on and the curtains open. I let myself in and call Alice's name. I shout up the stairs, leaping up two at a time, I sense something is wrong. No Alice. I return downstairs into the kitchen. At first, I don't see her, the lights on, there is a cup with a teabag waiting to be made. I call out again, then my eye sees Alice's foot, it's wedged between the bathroom and backdoor. Panic. "Alice, Alice oh my God, Alice". I look at her crumpled body, her head has been bleeding its now dried in congealed rivulets down her face and neck, her eyes are closed. I think she is dead. My hands shake as I use my phone, I dial 999, a calm voice asks which service I require, I switch to automatic pilot, give the operator the information. I follow her guidance to check for a pulse, yes, I think I feel one I'm not sure, my heart is racing, the blood is pumping through my veins. I place Alice into the recovery position, I wonder why I can't remember the training for CPR. I listen, yes there is definitely a heartbeat, its faint but she is alive. Ten minutes seems like an hour, the ambulance man is hammering on the front door, I let them in. They check Alice, wrapping her in a special blanket, "This ladies very cold, do we know how long she has been lying here?" I shake my head. I agree to follow the ambulance to the hospital to help with paperwork and advise of medical history. Before I leave, I make the house secure, collect Alice's medication and telephone the office so they can arrange cover for my other calls. Then I drive to Accident and Emergency. At the hospital the Nurse informs me Alice is stable but not quite out of danger yet. Of course, her age and her pre-existing conditions will affect her ability to pull through. I decide to ring Johnnie, he needs to know about his mother.

Johnnie is full of questions, why, when what, who. No one knew how long Alice had been outside, staff had called at nine o clock the previous evening, to give Alice her cocoa and medication. Although Alice had been upset at lunch time, she appeared calm and chatty at the tea call. What had upset her? What did the Doctor say? Who found her? I answered all of Johnnie's questions as accurately as I could. I wasn't sure who made the nine o'clock call I would make enquiries. He explains that he can't come over today, but he will ring the hospital later to check how is mother is. He probably wouldn't be able to get over tomorrow, Friday is a very busy day. Johnnie rang off after ensuring I was aware of his total commitment to his mother's welfare, although he did have a wife and two children who also needed him. Not to mention the work commitments. He will definitely come over on Saturday.

Back in the office I can't find a seat, Alan is hanging out in the kitchen, we both agree how ridiculous it is not to be able to sit down and decide to take a coffee break next door. Once seated Alan has an announcement to make, he is about to become a Granddad for the third time, he's very excited, they are a close family. I have two grandchildren, unfortunately, I rarely get to see them. They live quite close but with work commitments, school and various other excuses I just don't see them. Of course, this will be worse next month when they move away, across to Liverpool. They have found a house there with a garden and my son has already got a transfer from the company he works for, selling mobile phones.

Alan tells me he's working on a new case, a young man of twenty-six, who was employed at a Bank, had good prospects, bought a house, car all the usual consumer products. Now he's lost his job, been in trouble with the police and is known to be addicted to sniffing glue and gases. His house, which is about to be repossessed, was full of empty gas aerosols when Alan visited. Alan looked sad, "Thing is Carla, he's a really nice lad. He reminds me of my son, he had so much going for him. Now he has well and truly lost his way, in with a bad crowd. I think they've taken money off him. They have obviously been having 'Sniffing Parties' at his house, the place was a mess when I called. I'm hoping to get him re-housed."

We both have experience with the Drugs and Alcohol team and are familiar with the problems associated with this form of addiction. There are several ways in which the gasses can be inhaled, but its difficult for the user to control the dose, and all methods can be fatal. The effects of 'sniffing' can be a little like being drunk, sometimes with fits of laughter and inability to think logically. The results of taking these gases can be debilitating, mood swings and hallucinations. The users often display aggressive behaviour and are physically ill, vomiting and sometimes having blackouts.

Alan smiles, "Onwards and upwards, best be getting back, maybe I can get a computer now. Got an appointment with John from the D&A team and Paul from housing this afternoon." I wink at Alan, "Tell Paul not to work too hard, we have an appointment this evening". Paul and I have been seeing each other for over a year, usually a couple of times a week. We are planning a little holiday together this summer, I'm pretty nervous and very excited about it, a Greek island sounds brilliant.

Visit Two Weeks Later

Alice left hospital one week ago, Johnnie her son rang to inform me Alice is now in a residential care home and would not be needing any further support. He reluctantly gave me the name of the care home but suggested I didn't visit, to allow Alice time to settle in. Alice had not been happy about moving and he didn't want her to be upset by my visit. Technically then Alice was no longer my case, but I wanted to sign her off officially, so I went on my day off to find the care home.

It wasn't as bad as I had anticipated, a large Victorian house in its own grounds and it had been extended to include additional bedrooms and a large conservatory. Upon arrival I ask for the manager, as I am led through the house I scan around for Alice. The manager assumes I'm a relative, "Oh, thank goodness you have come, I have been trying to contact John, her son, for a week now. Did you bring the things?" He stares at the small carrier bag I am carrying. He's a small man. Around mid-fifties, going bald with a too obvious comb over and thick glasses. He and his wife established the home three years ago. "We don't have the skills and staff to deal with dementia client's here, I did explain that to John, he said his mother was just recovering from a fall. He didn't leave her enough clothes. My wife has sorted her some nightdresses, but with her incontinence issues we are going to need more clothes and personal toiletries". I explain that I was Alice's support worker and had come along to see how she had settled in. "Oh, great, do you know if she has ever been diagnosed for dementia?" he asked, pushing his glasses further up his nose. "Only we are experiencing a lot of difficulties with Alice, especially at night. John promised to forward any relevant paperwork, but we've not heard from him since and is phone is out of service."

I spend the next hour going through Alice's case history, providing details of her GP and her current medication. Which of course, she has not been taking since her arrival. I am shocked that Alice appears to have just been abandoned here, with few belongings, no medication and no case history. Mr Gordon the Manager asks if I think we need to contact the police, he doesn't feel they are able to care for Alice for much longer. I ask to see Alice.

We go up to the first floor, along a corridor to the room. Alice is sat in an armchair gazing out of the window. The room is small but clean, a single bed, chest of drawer, small bookcase with a lamp on. A small bathroom, wet room, is in the far corner. The window looks out over the concrete car park.

"Hello, Alice how are you. It's Carla". I look at Alice, she doesn't respond. "She as lost a lot of weight since I last saw her". I say to Mr Gordon, just as a passing observation, he responds immediately, "She will not eat, throws her food on the floor and disrupts the entire dining room, quite honestly mealtimes are a nightmare, most evenings she refuses to even come to the dining room.". I look at Alice, so frail, so detached. "Alice is used to eating alone, could she not have meals in her room?" Its a suggestion I offer to try and help.

"No, we don't do room service. All our residents come to the dining room for all meals. If we started room service for one, we would have to do it for everyone. I have been trying to reach John, Mr De Costa to tell him he must find alternative accommodation for his mother, we just can't cope." Mr Gordon has removed his glasses and is wiping them on a handkerchief. I make a decision, "Its Friday today, can I have till next week to sort this? I will bring Alice some toiletries and a change of outfit tomorrow, I need to try and find the elusive John and sort out somewhere for Alice". Reluctantly he agrees, I'm not sure what I'm going to do but I have the weekend to formulate a plan. I try to speak to Alice again, but she is just staring into space, watching the car park. As we leave Alice whispers, "He's back again, he found me".

Alice remembered Johnnie coming to see her, she had been in hospital where those nice nurses looked after her, her head and her leg were sore, she wasn't sure how that happened. Now, what did Johnnie say, something about a nice hotel, a little holiday for her. He said he would bring Stewart to see her. This place, it wasn't home, Alice wanted to go home. It was a hotel, but Alice didn't want to stay here. There were too many old people. It was too noisy, to hot, too many people. Were they nurses? Telling her when to get dressed, get undressed, get washed. She was Alice De Costa and had been getting herself up, washed and dressed since she was five. Who was that young woman her voice sounded familiar??

That evening Paul and I shared a lovely meal at the local curry house, we both enjoy spicy food. We laugh, chat about childhood mishaps, Paul explains his miss-spent youth, when one Friday, he had too much to drink, jumped on the last train home. Only to fall asleep and wake up over sixty miles away, in some remote station, where there were no further trains until Monday. He then had to ring his mother at one in the morning and ask her to come and get him. That was twenty years ago, his mother still referred to it when lecturing on the risks of too much alcohol. As the evening wore on, work crept into the conversation, without using names I tell Paul about the scenario with Alice. Paul suggests the best route is through the police who could track the son down, Paul also recommends another home which specialises in dementia care. It is a lovely evening, we enjoy each other's company, though neither of us mention commitment or love, we were just as they say, friends with benefits.

The following day I took Alice some clothes and toiletries, I managed to find two skirts that had belonged to my daughter and a couple of nice tee shirts were donated by my mother. Everything would probably be big, but they were clean and tidy. I also decided to sneak some food in, I took a home made ham and salad sandwich on brown bread and a thick and creamy strawberry yoghurt. At the home Mr Gordon is out but his wife Rosemary takes me to see Alice, we exchange, a few words about the weather, then Rosemary leaves, saying something about needing to get a crumble in the oven. I put the clothes away for Alice, who is still wearing the same outfit as yesterday, which makes me wonder if they had actually got her to go to bed. I then offer Alice the sandwich, to my surprise Alice eats the sandwich, then points at the yoghurt. Damn, I have forgotten a spoon. I quickly go down to the dining room and sneak out a spoon. Alice eats her yoghurt.

Monday morning, Bill is waiting for me, "What's happening with Alice, I got your text on Friday. Is she still in the home?" Bill is never pleased when I get too involved, take things over the line as he puts it. I explain the events over the last three days and my plan. Bill listens, then surprises me by saying, "OK, go ahead. If he has just abandoned his mother well, lets wait and see could be a genuine reason, keep me in the picture. Oh, and put in a claim for the stuff you bought." I grin, part relief and part respect, Bill did have a big heart he just tried to hide it."

I inform the police of the missing person or possible missing family, the situation regarding Alice and the need to get her the correct care. The police are very sympathetic, dismayed that a son could do this. The address we have for the son is empty, neighbours say the family moved away, one night about a week ago, no one knew where. The house was rented, and Mr De Costa left owing nearly two thousand pounds in rent arrears. A missing person alert was distributed Nationwide. A meeting is organised, it is agreed that a place will be sought at the Dementia Care home. The police had visited Alice's old house, which was also rented from the council. The remains of Alice's belonging would be held for a short time then if not claimed disposed of. I didn't think Alice would want anything, but I managed to get her photographs and some clothes before the council moved in.

Mr Gordon was extremely pleased to hear the news, Alice's midnight wanderings it appeared upset all the residents, her screams of abuse towards an unknown person kept everyone awake. By Friday I was able to collect Alice, who seemed excited to be going out, Alice looked even thinner and I requested a medical check up for her. The new home is much quieter, I take Alice's hand as we go through the door. The doors are all coded to prevent 'wandering', the staff are trained in dementia care, the Senior Carer meets us and shows us to her room. Its on the ground floor overlooking the garden, she has a bed, cupboard, table and an easy chair. I have been and placed all Alice's photos on the cupboard. Alice looks at the pictures, then turns. "Do I know you? Are you a friend of Joes?" she asks the Senior Carer. "I'm not sure who is Joe Alice?" Alice gazes at the pictures "He's someone I used to know I think."

Alice settles into her new home, she takes part in the daily activities and eats a little more. The staff coax her to visit the internal hairdresser and now she has a new hair style. Alice still has her hallucinations but with care and medication she copes. A medical examination reveals Alice has stage 4 Hodgkin Lymphoma, she is blissfully unaware. We never heard from John or his family again.

ABOUT THE AUTHOR

Carole Parker, born in Lancashire in 1955, I grew up in Greater Manchester. In 1979 I moved to the South of England where I lived for twenty years.

I have always wanted to write and forty years ago I wrote two articles which were published. Unfortunately life events take over. I now have to adult children and three grandchildren. Over the years I have also fostered eighteen children, including teenagers. In 2016 I visited the Greek island of Syros, where I purchased a Greek farmhouse, in need of restoration. I spend must of my free time painting and writing.

I spent ten years working in various departments within Social Services, which has been the inspiration for my book. This is my first attempt at writing and self publishing, a major achievement for someone who is not technically skilled.

Printed in Poland
by Amazon Fulfillment
Poland Sp. z o.o., Wrocław